Chesapeake Crimes II

Chesapeake Crimes II

Coordinating Editors
Donna Andrews and Maria Y. Lima

Editorial Panel
Trish Carrico, Patrick Hyde,
and Maria Y. Lima

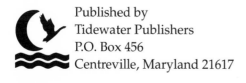

Published by
Tidewater Publishers
P.O. Box 456
Centreville, Maryland 21617

Library of Congress Cataloging-in-Publication Data
Chesapeake crimes II / coordinating editors, Donna Andrews
and Maria Lima.
   p. cm.
  ISBN-13: 978-0-87033-582-2
  1. Detective and mystery stories, American. 2. American fiction-
-Women authors. I. Andrews, Donna. II. Lima, Maria Y.
PS648.D4C46 2006
813'.08720835--dc22
2006029924

Contributors

Goodie Cantwell

Nora Charles

Leone Ciporin

Carla Coupe

Elizabeth Foxwell

Chris Freeburn

Barb Goffman

Peggy Hanson

G. M. Malliet

Sherriel Mattingly

Valerie O. Patterson

Judy Pomeranz

Harriette I. Sackler

Marcia Talley

Sandi Wilson

Table of Contents

Table of Contents

Foreword 1

Smart Enough by Goodie Cantwell 3

A Senior Discount on Death by Nora Charles 14

A Rose by Any Other Name by Leone Ciporin 24

Rear View Murder by Carla Coupe 32

The Last to Know by Elizabeth Foxwell 42

Dying for a Clue by Chris Freeburn 48

Murder at Sleuthfest by Barb Goffman 66

Death in the Aegean: An Elizabeth Darcy
Adventure by Peggy Hanson 70

The Bartender by G. M. Malliet 84

The Pink Sweater by Sherriel Mattingly 96

Death in Woad Blue by Valerie O. Patterson 103

The Cozy Caprice by Judy Pomeranz 111

Mother Love by Harriette I. Sackler 123

Driven to Distraction by Marcia Talley 132

The Blonde in Black by Sandi Wilson 144

Foreword
by Donna Andrews

We have a remarkable number of good mystery writers here in. . . and at this point my foreword-writing stalled for a while, as I tried to come up with a succinct yet accurate term for exactly what "here" is.

The national capital area? Sounds rather grand, and I have a theory that the proximity of the federal government may help explain why so many local writers feel inspired to murder—if only on paper. But that does rather leave out the contributors who hail from, say, Annapolis and West Virginia. Same problem with "Baltimore/Washington area." I could say that our contributors come from Maryland, Virginia, West Virginia, and the District of Columbia, but that's not very catchy, is it?

The common thread that holds these fifteen writers together is that they're all passionate enough about mysteries to have joined the Chesapeake Chapter of Sisters in Crime. They all trek as often as they can to wherever this month's chapter meeting will take place. And they've all agreed to donate their stories to the Chesapeake Crimes II anthology, whose proceeds, like those of the original Chesapeake Crimes, will go to support the chapter's activities.

So maybe that's the catchy phrase I was looking for. We're the Chesapeake Crime Scene.

And now I'll shut up and let the stories speak for themselves.

Smart Enough
by Goodie Cantwell

Not smart. Tonight she had made a mistake. Helen Congers knew that. It would have been so easy to tell Sally just to go home when she showed up two hours late. Those were the rules. Then Helen would be leafing through a magazine in the warm, well-lit nursing station of Bentler's Home for the Aged, earning overtime plus a commendation. Instead she was inching down Route 10 in the darkness with her hazards flashing while the rain pounded on the windshield. No matter how she adjusted her thick glasses, she could barely make out the road in front of her. It must be nearly three.

Helen began to hum softly, something she always did when she was tense. Her parents had told her not to be a patsy. She'd always known she wasn't the brightest light on the porch. Shouldn't have bothered, she thought ruefully, her parents always seemed to get so much pleasure reminding her.

"Girl, I'm not certain your elevator ever gets to the top floor." Her father, all six feet two of him, would lean over laughing and give her a hug. "Don't worry, you wouldn't know what to do if you got there."

"Oh, leave her alone. She can't help it." Mom would sigh. "It's her looks that worry me. Now I come from a long line of lookers. I think she takes after your mother."

Their image was crystal clear in her mind. The two of them sitting on the sofa, oddly unified, looking at her and shaking their heads, the unspoken being spoken, "What will happen to her when we are gone?"

When they died, she'd missed them all the time. Now it was just now and then. Dad had been a bear of a man and strode out of life with gusto. It was as if he had been in a big hurry. Mom, once he was gone, just sort of shriveled up and drifted slowly away like a butterfly disintegrating in the wind.

Helen had taken good care of them, all the way through. She was proud of that. The visiting nurse had said she was blessed with gentle, healing hands. She thought her parents would have been surprised how things had worked out. She'd learned how to drive. They'd always said she would never be able to do that. Finding the job at Bentler's had been a snap. Taking care of them had given her all the training she needed.

The job was wonderful. She'd just put a copy of her latest performance evaluation on the refrigerator. "Helen tackles any job. She's got a good attitude. Keeps quiet and works hard." Even Buddy had seemed impressed.

The rain slackened. She stopped humming. It was only a few moments before a sign loomed on the right proclaiming Frankmont Cooperatives to be the Best Bargain in Town. As she turned onto the small access road that ran to the parking lot behind her apartment, she felt genuinely relieved. She was home.

This complex had been called an architect's bad dream from the fifties, but Helen didn't care. She loved the way its two-story brick houses clustered with shared entranceways and stoops. Everyone minded everyone else's business. No need to read the newspaper, just ask the magpies. That's what Helen had named the old ladies who sat on the steps or peered out their windows, keeping track of everything that happened, or didn't happen for that matter.

As she locked her car, Helen shivered. Being alone in the cold, wet, dark night made her nervous. She tried to cheer herself thinking of Buddy sitting in the kitchen window, waiting for her, all black except for his feet and his tuxedo chest.

Not her lucky night. There was Lew Jones doing his nightly stagger returning from Dempsey's Bar and Grill. She looked at her watch. It was just three. The rain hadn't slowed him a bit. He was right on schedule—she was the one who was late. He made an odd picture, an elf of a man, short and wiry, lurching across the parking lot toward her.

"Hi, Helen," he called out.

"Good evening, Mr. Jones." Helen answered.

"Oh, aren't we formal tonight," Jones said as he caught up with her. "Call me Lew. Wouldn't hurt you to be friendly."

"It wouldn't hurt you to do something about getting that fixed." Helen stopped and pointed to the storm drain with its crumbling cement. They both turned and faced the hole. It was quiet for a moment as they watched the water rush down.

"Not my problem. It's the county's job."

"It's dangerous. You're the maintenance man here. They'll come if you call." Something about Jones made Helen feel nervous and she moved away from him.

"It's ugly, but not dangerous." Jones stepped right next to her. Their shoulders were almost touching.

"If we had a bad storm and someone slipped, they could get swept down there."

Jones laughed. "Nonsense, no one's going to walk over there." He gave her a smile she didn't like. "But listen, I'll call tomorrow. Don't want you worrying your pretty little head off your shoulders about it."

What was Jones up to? No one had ever referred to her head as pretty.

"How about a reward, Helen?" He reeked of liquor. "You should come and have a drink with me sometime."

"Thank you, but I don't drink, Mr. Jones," she said stonily and stepped away from him.

"As far as I can see, you don't do much of anything except hang out with that fool cat of yours."

"My social life is just fine." Actually it wasn't, but that was none of his business. She sounded defensive and hated herself for it.

"It would be good for you to get out a little bit," Jones edged closer to her. "You can be friendly. I saw you with that Frank Klinger out in the back under the trees last summer."

Helen could feel her cheeks flush. How did he know about that? "Well, I'm not going to be friendly with you." She turned and started to walk home.

"Just think about it. That Frank dropped you fast enough, and my old lady won't give me anything anymore." Somehow Jones had moved in front of her. "You must have needs."

"No need of you."

She could see she'd made him angry. As she started to walk around him, he made a half-hearted lunge at her. She grabbed his arm and twisted it, just like she learned in the self-defense class at the Y. It had been worth the money.

"Ouch, you little bitch." Jones pulled back, rubbing his arm. "You shouldn't be so picky. It's not like you're anything to look at. I just figured if I kept my eyes shut, it wouldn't be too bad."

"You're a creep." Helen walked faster. She wanted to slug him. "I'll tell your wife."

"She won't believe you." Jones followed her.

He was probably right about that. There was no point in telling anyone. No one would believe her.

Home was just 30 feet away. She could see Buddy's white chest in the window.

"And that cat of yours. It's got to go. You know the rules. No pets."

Suddenly he had power. She felt panic. "Buddy was here before the bylaws were amended. He's. . ." she searched for the word, "granddaddied."

"Don't count on it. And remember, if anything happens to him, you can't have another one."

"My cat's in all the time, he never bothers anybody or anything," she said over her shoulder as she got her keys and started up her walk.

Jones grabbed her arm and this time, frozen with dread, she did not resist. He leaned forward and she smelled the liquor on his breath.

"Remember, call me Lew, Helen. It's all very easy. I'll be nice to your kitty, if your pussy's nice to me."

Nothing happened for the next few weeks. Helen went back to working days, which she liked better anyway. Some of the other aides hated to work days. The old folks were more troublesome and the relatives would visit and start making complaints. Helen enjoyed the commotion and the squabbles.

She was busy sorting out the laundry caper when they called her to the phone. Mrs. Swartz had Mrs. Smith's clothes and Mrs. Smith had some of Mrs. Swartz's plus some garments whose owner had yet to be identified. Each of the old ladies was convinced the other had taken her things.

"Congers, telephone," rang down the hall.

Helen couldn't believe it. No one even had the number here.

It was one of the magpies. "Helen, it took me forever to find you. I didn't know for certain which nursing home you worked for. I had to call information and then just start with the As." The old woman paused to catch her breath. "Lucky you work for Bentler's. I could have been looking for you all afternoon."

Helen broke in. "Why did you call, Mrs. Crosby?"

"Oh, it's your cat. Horrible screech. Happened right after Mr. Jones went into your house."

"He can't just walk into my house." Helen's voice raised and her grip on the phone tightened.

"Well, he said there was a problem with the gas. He was mad when he came out. Your cat really scratched him. Said your cat was vicious and ought to be put to sleep."

"That's ridiculous, a big man like that and a little cat." Helen's sense of anger gave way to fear. "Is Buddy okay?"

"Well, that's why I called. Mrs. McCabe and I went over and looked in the window. You don't mind do you? We didn't want to snoop, just wanted to see if he was okay."

Helen forced herself to be calm. "Did you see him?"

"No, we didn't. And you know he's such a friendly little thing. If you bang on the window, he'll come right over. So we decided to call you."

How odd, Helen thought, that these old ladies had been tapping on her window and playing with her cat, and she'd never known it. "I think I better come home."

"Maybe you shouldn't. Mr. Jones may have just stepped on his tail. You know how cats can holler. And they do sleep during the day." Mrs. Crosby was sounding more and more uncertain. "Maybe I shouldn't have called you. Wouldn't want you to have trouble on your job."

"I won't get in trouble at work. I'm coming home right now." Helen hung up the receiver before the old lady could respond.

She got home in fifteen minutes. Mrs. Crosby and Mrs. McCabe were waiting by her front door. Everything was oddly quiet when they entered the house. Helen called Buddy, quietly at first and then more loudly. She could feel the panic rising in her voice. He didn't answer. Then she began to mew, at first very softly, but her pitch rose and the tempo of her calls increased. Mrs. Crosby and Mrs. McCabe exchanged nervous glances.

Then she heard it. A faint moan from under the sofa. She dropped to her hands and knees. She could barely make out Buddy's eyes blinking at her. He was back toward the wall.

"Come on, Buddy," she cooed.

He didn't move. She continued to cajole, but the cat just lay looking at her.

She got to her feet. "We got to get him out."

"Sometimes they crawl off to die." Mrs. McCabe shook her head in a knowing fashion. "It might be kindest just to leave him."

Helen repeated. "We got to get him out."

"Come on, Mabel," Mrs. Crosby said. "She's right."

When Helen looked back at it later on, it had been truly amazing. Once those two old ladies had decided to move the sofa, it had been a snap. She was surprised how strong they were, a pair of elderly amazons.

She knelt down next to Buddy. Lying there, he looked so tiny and frail. She thought his eyes were accusing her. At least he was breathing. She felt an overwhelming sense of loss.

Mrs. Crosby had tears in her eyes. "Oh, look at the poor thing. It's his back legs. I wonder how he did that. Do you think they're broken?"

"More like dislocated." Mrs. McCabe patted Helen on the back. "You're going to have to put him down."

Helen walked outside into a beautiful morning. The March rains had passed and daffodils were everywhere. Crosby and McCabe stood on the sidewalk. They'd become her friends in the three weeks since that horrible moment with Buddy. It looked as if they were waiting for her.

"Before you look at the headlines on that paper, Helen you'd better get a grip. Jones's popped up." Mrs. Crosby said. Her normally cheerful face was serious.

"Popped up?" was the only comment Helen could muster.

"His body. In the middle of the river." Mrs. McCabe nodded.

"Dead?"

"Of course, he's dead. It's like we guessed," Mrs. McCabe said. "He must have slipped down that broken drain coming home from Dempsey's the night of that big storm and blackout last week. The night he disappeared."

All Helen felt was relief.

Mrs. Crosby said, "He's a real mess, they say. Got totally mangled in the drains."

"Horrible to think of him down there." Helen shuddered. "He must've got stuck."

Mrs. McCabe peered at Helen with a quizzical look. "Didn't think you liked him much after what he did to your cat."

"I didn't," Helen said emphatically. "In fact, I hated him. But this is too awful."

"At least the family will have some closure now." A sudden ruthless glint crept into Mrs. Crosby's eyes. "Plus they'll be able to sue the county for a bundle."

"There will be a big fight." Mrs. McCabe set her lips in a determined line. "The county guys had come and put up all that yellow tape around the hole that afternoon. They'll say he was negligent. He was drunk, of course, but I still don't see how he managed to walk into that hole."

"Me neither," Helen said. "I gave it a wide berth when I came home that night. He must have walked right over the yellow tape."

"He had to have seen it. You saw it," Mrs. McCabe said. "I saw how it was hanging the next morning, a little messed up by the storm, but still up."

"Maybe, he just ignored it." Helen paused, pretending to think. "I remember him telling me the drain wasn't dangerous. I told him it was. Someone could get hurt." She hoped she wasn't talking too much.

"Well he was wrong."

Dead wrong, Helen thought.

Mrs. McCabe got a faraway look for a moment, but then she came back focused. "Let's not talk about Jones anymore. I hate to speak ill of the dead, but he was a nasty man. Let's talk about something pleasant."

Mrs. Crosby brightened. "I see you got your cat back day before yesterday. How is he?"

"He's good, but he'll always have a limp." Buddy was not quite the same. The cat seemed lethargic, didn't want to play with his toys anymore. It's only temporary was what the vet had said.

"It was good to see him in your window." There was hope in Mrs. Crosby's eyes. "Bet that doctoring cost you a bundle."

"It did, but he's my family." Helen had decided how much Buddy's treatment had cost was going to remain her secret.

Mrs. McCabe looked at Helen speculatively. "You used to have such a hangdog look, but now you just seem to be ready for anything."

Helen laughed. "I think it's just that now I know I can take care of things. All sorts of things."

"You're nobody's fool, Helen," Mrs. McCabe said. "You never were."

She wasn't as smart as the magpies thought she was, Helen told herself once she got back in the house. She fingered the piece of knotted yellow tape in her pocket. She'd forgotten all about it. Why hadn't she just dropped it in the water? It would have gone right down the storm drain.

That night had been so dark with the blackout and the storm. Jones was going to be there any minute. She couldn't get the tape untied. Odd how Mom's advice would pay off. She'd always said carry nail scissors just in case. Somehow, Helen thought this was not the sort of use her mother had in mind. One snip was all it took. Then she stood back in the shadows, holding the yellow tape tightly in her hands. Very simple really, to just route him the wrong way.

Helen turned the knotted yellow tape over. She'd had to cut off this piece. Someone might have noticed if there had been two knots. Putting the tape back up had been a lot harder than taking it down. McCabe was right. It hadn't looked the same.

Now the problem was how to get rid of it? If she flushed it and it clogged the pipes, how could she explain that? If she threw it away outside her house, someone might notice. Helen began to hum.

The humming stopped. She grabbed her nail scissors and cut the tape into very thin strips. She got her knitting needles and some yellow wool from her basket. Within an hour she had interwoven the wool and yellow strips into a nice cat toy. She held it out at arm's length. It was really rather attractive.

Helen sprinkled some catnip on her creation. She tossed it on the floor. "Come on, Buddy, see the nice fat rat I've made for you."

The cat sniffed the toy cautiously and started batting it around. Gradually he became more interested, pouncing on it. Finally he was rolling over and over, clutching it with his paws. Helen was relieved. It was good to see that he still knew how to play.

She smiled. "Buddy, we won't call it Rat, we'll call it Jonesey."

Old enough to remember the Korean War and young enough to have worn the first miniskirt in Moscow, Goodie Cantwell works in the Office of Information Technology at American University. She lived with her husband, a journalist, and her two children in New York City, London, Moscow, and Prague. Now a widow, Goodie lives in Bethesda, Maryland, with two clueless cats, and has just finished her first mystery, Walking the Dog Can Be Dangerous.

A Senior Discount On Death
by Nora Charles

Well, she'd earned every wrinkle Kate Kennedy decided, applying SPF 40 sunblock to her cheeks a half century too late. The damage done decades ago, during those carefree summers at Rockaway, another beach on the Atlantic Ocean, back when everyone believed direct exposure to morning sunshine was good for all God's creatures.

Swiping her greasy fingers with a Wipe & Dry—too fastidious even by her own standards—Kate returned to the *Sun-Sentinel's* article about a Cuban drowning while trying to reach Florida. Such a handsome young man. So sad.

"Do you think I'll ever get my gusto back?" Marlene Friedman, in a plus size scarlet tankini, shifted her chair to catch the sun's rays on her already tanned-to-toast shoulders. "My lust for life has been slipping away for months— you must have noticed—now it's gone with the wind."

Kate smiled, noting Marlene had used two movie titles to describe her loss. They'd spent most of their childhood Saturdays at double features.

"As my best friend and former sister-in-law, you have a moral obligation to help me find it again."

Kate—convinced that more than a few of those lines on her face were the direct result of Marlene's bright ideas— sighed, stalling, wanting to support and dissuade simultaneously. No easy trick.

"Look, you haven't lost your gusto, but even if you had, why would taking sailing lessons help get it back?" Kate's stomach churned in the all-too-familiar Pepcid AC alert that Marlene's schemes often generated.

"Not lessons, Kate. Holiday USA has invited us to spend a day aboard a thirty-six foot motor/sailboat, and, yes, we can take the wheel or hoist the jib, while deciding if we'd like to become one of its part-time sailors/owners."

"Sounds like a scam to me." They sat in their striped beach chairs planted at the water's edge, with warm surf washing over their feet. Kate arched her toes in pleasure and took a deep breath of the sharp, salt air. "Whoever heard of timeshares on a sailboat?"

"Scam?" Marlene's laughter certainly seemed as lusty as ever. "We're former New Yorkers, too old and too smart to scam, right? All we have to do is listen to an hour-long Holiday USA timeshare presentation. In return, we get to cruise up the Intercoastal and out to the ocean, maybe do some deep sea fishing or sit back and sip a Cosmo. Who knows, an attractive man might be on deck."

Kate suppressed a giggle: Gusto gone, huh?

"Come on, Kate. The voyage is limited to six passengers..."

"Prospects. We won't be guests on a private yacht, Marlene. You filled in a Holiday USA promotion form you found on the counter in the dry cleaners."

"Okay, prospects. But their sales office and pier are located on the beach side of the Intercoastal, so we can walk there. The ship sails at noon. And we get a free lunch onboard."

The free lunch closed the deal for Kate.

They met at 11:30 in Ocean Vista's ornate, bordering on gaudy, lobby. Marlene's nautical attire reminded Kate of Carol Channing on Broadway in *Gentlemen Prefer Blondes*. However, knowing they'd be sailing into the wind, she'd arranged her platinum hair in a sleek French twist.

Kate wore boat shoes, khakis, and a white shirt with the sleeves rolled up.

She'd moved into Ocean Vista nine months ago on the same day that her husband, Charlie, had dropped dead still clutching the pen he'd used to close on the condo. She missed Charlie and their decades of pillow talk about his cases as a NYPD Homicide Detective. And she missed her family up in New York, especially her granddaughters.

South Florida's relentless sunshine still depressed her, but with Marlene two floors below, and Charlie's beloved Westie, Ballou, as her beach-walking companion, Kate had—ever so cautiously—begun to think of Palmetto Beach as home.

In the February midday sun, as they walked the one long block north along A1A to Neptune Boulevard, Kate took time to both see and smell the flowers: a riot of fuchsia and purple hibiscus and jasmine so sweet its aroma embraced you like a lover.

Senior citizens tended to arrive early. As they approached the Holiday USA berth on the Intercoastal pier, Kate spotted her shipmates queuing near a rope ladder at the aft of the boat.

Good. That meant they wouldn't be going into the office for a preliminary sales pitch. But why were so few prospects boarding a 36-foot boat?

The white double-ender appeared sleek and yar. Kate had done some sailing off Shelter Island years ago and learned the lingo. While she could handle the wheel and, being the smallest onboard, had been hoisted up to the crow's nest to adjust a line, she failed knot tying, and when she tried to work the sails, they'd flapped around her face.

Still...she felt a sudden rush of excitement, a shiver of anticipation.

"We can't be this bloody low on gas. Where the hell did those landlubbers from Ohio motor out to last night?" A crusty old salt, in dirty shorts straining to cover his wide bottom and sporting a stained captain's hat, shouted down from the bow, addressing another old guy—this one toned, tanned, and impeccably dressed in yachting white—on the dock.

The walking/talking Ralph Lauren ad looked angry, but only for a fleeting moment, before he turned from the captain and flashed thirty thousand dollars worth of dazzlingly white, capped teeth at Kate and Marlene.

"Good afternoon. According to the manifest, you must be Ms. Friedman and Mrs. Kennedy. I'm your Holiday USA host, Clive Weber. Welcome. Let me help you aboard the *Shady Lady.*"

Weber spoke with a gushing Texas accent, his hand clamped on Kate's shoulder. She squirmed free, her instant dislike accompanied by an odd feeling of unease.

A handsome, silver-haired Latino stood off to the side, observing. He caught her eye, glanced at Weber, turned back to Kate, and nodded. Had he read her mind?

A couple in matching baby blue jogging suits, whom Clive Weber introduced as the Daltons, were boarding, climbing the rope ladder with great difficulty: the captain pulling, the host pushing.

"Senor Martinez, your wife isn't with you?" Weber checked his manifest.

"Regretfully, no." Martinez smiled at Kate and Marlene. "Please call me Juan," he said, then scampered up the ladder like a teenage athlete.

Clive Weber's unnecessary boost to her rear landed Kate on deck.

Despite her girth, Marlene, a former Olympic swimmer, navigated the ladder with ease.

And, moments later, they were motoring toward the Deerfield Beach Inlet where they would enter the Atlantic Ocean and raise the *Shady Lady*'s sails.

It occurred to Kate that all seven onboard, the captain, the host, and the five passengers, were over sixty. Ship of Old Fools? Maybe.

Kate, Marlene, and Connie Dalton, a chatty gal with apple cheeks and a sunny smile, helped Clive Weber serve an excellent catered lunch. Everyone, except Juan, who mostly smiled and nodded, and made easy small talk.

Connie's husband, Bob, as plump and pleasant as his wife, cleaned up, stuffing used paper plates in big garbage bags, while the ladies stowed the leftovers in the tiny fridge.

The smell of coffee drifting up from the galley made Kate again wonder why she, a confirmed tea drinker, so loved coffee's aroma, but not its taste.

Captain Mike—Clive Weber hadn't mentioned his surname—seemingly over his snit about the diminished fuel in his tank, was pointing out the mansions lining the Intercoastal, regaling his passengers with stories about their famous and infamous past owners.

As Connie applauded, Kate's feeling of unease surfaced again.

When the *Shady Lady* reached the inlet, the captain veered north, and Clive Weber stood in the bow and started his sales pitch. "As Holiday USA's 'specially selected guests,' y'all are entitled to a senior discount. How about that, folks? All the joys of boat ownership, but none of the worries." Weber, his drawl thick as oil, pointed to the matching jogging suits. "Now, Bob and Connie, here, might reserve the *Shady Lady* for Tuesday mornings from 8 to 12, then we'd scrub down the deck and you lovely ladies," he gestured to Kate and Marlene, "would come aboard that afternoon from 1 to 4. While we're sailing, just think about owning a piece of this beautiful boat."

No mention of what a timeshare might cost. That would come at the close. Kate bet Clive Weber was a great closer and that he'd once worked as a telemarketer. Since the FCC's ban on unsolicited calls, many telemarketers had moved on to other unsavory sales positions. Boat time-shares would have been a natural segue.

The captain steered into the eye of the wind and Clive Weber raised the jib.

Kate settled back on the port cushions and, while the *Shady Lady* rode the waves with style and grace, watched the navy blue sea seeming to kiss the muted terra cotta horizon.

She did not spot the gun until Juan Martinez pulled it out of his breast pocket and pointed it at Clive Weber. Certainly the .25 caliber pistol had not made even the slightest bulge in his white nylon windbreaker.

"Please change course, immediately," the soft-spoken Martinez ordered the captain in his slightly accented English. Then he pressed the pistol against Weber's right temple. "Head southeast to Cuba."

Connie Dalton screamed. Clive, shaking, dropped the jib line and the sheet flapped wildly in the wind, knocking Bob Dalton to his knees. Kate glanced at Marlene who rose from the cushioned seat on the port side, poised to move. Kate shook her head, warning her former sister-in-law not to try anything foolish.

"No one will be hurt if you do as I say." Juan Martinez's voice, icy polite and soft, scared Kate more than the pistol. "We're going to pick up my cousins. Now change course, Captain, or I will shoot Mr. Weber." Martinez kicked Bob Dalton. "Get up, Mr. Dalton, and grab the line before we list too far to starboard."

For a split second everyone seemed frozen in place.

Kate watched in mounting horror, sensing the scene had been choreographed and she wasn't one of the players. *Ship of Fools*. Hadn't they all died? No...maybe that was *The Flying Dutchman.*

The wind whipped up, bringing bigger waves, tossing the double-ender around in the rough sea. In typical Florida fashion, the weather suddenly had changed and they were in the middle of a wicked storm.

The captain turned the wheel hard to the right. Bob Dalton rose to his feet and reached for, but missed, the jib's line. The rain came, hammering the boat, and Marlene was flung across the deck. Crawling, Kate snatched the line, lowering the sail. Thank God they hadn't raised the main.

Out of nowhere, Connie Dalton charged forward, swinging a winch handle. A shot rang out. Though the handle had been aimed at Clive—had Connie gone crazy?—in the shifting, strong wind, it slammed into Juan Martinez's temple and he slid to the deck. Marlene, back on her feet, grabbed Martinez's gun, then screamed as Clive Weber went overboard.

Only then did Kate think it odd that none of them were wearing life jackets.

"Go radio the Coast Guard, Connie," Kate shouted over the wind. "Tell them we have a man overboard."

Captain Mike, struggling with the wheel, said, "The radio's broken, Mrs. Kennedy."

"Use your cell phone, Marlene."

"I doubt Ms. Friedman will get through. We're several miles out and the weather's bad." For a captain in danger of losing control of his boat, he sounded almost smug.

What the hell was going on here?

Marlene fumbled in her massive beach bag for the phone, finally finding it, only to realize the captain had been right. Not even a dial tone.

"Damn." She handed the gun to Kate, threw the phone on the deck seat, kicked off her shoes, and jumped over the starboard rail into the turbulent sea.

Marlene's ad-lib heroism gave the plot a new twist.

Kate aimed the gun at Bob and Connie. If this entire voyage had been staged, they were part of the act.

Juan sprawled on the deck, holding his bloody head.

"Down the hatch." Kate always wanted to use those words in some other context than trying to convince a toddler to eat. "You, too, Juan, get up."

The Daltons and a shaky Juan climbed down the ladder and she locked the cabin.

Know your characters, Kate thought. The authors of this charade hadn't been aware that Kate had practiced on the firing range with Charlie Kennedy for years. Nor had they known Marlene was a champion swimmer. Or that her big heart wouldn't allow even slime like Clive Weber to drown without making an effort to save him.

A few minutes passed in silence as the captain fought to keep the *Shady Lady* stable. An exhausted Marlene heaved herself over the railing. No Clive.

With the gun to his head, and fighting the rough sea, Captain Mike steered the *Shady Lady* back to Palmetto Beach.

"Look, dead ahead. There's the lighthouse," Marlene shouted. They entered the inlet, the rain stopped, the wind abated, and Kate reached the Coast Guard.

"Even when you two aren't playing Miss Marple, trouble just leaps into your laps, doesn't it?" Palmetto Beach Homicide Detective Nick Carbone frowned.

Carbone, less than a friend, yet more than a colleague in crime solving, and Kate had investigated (though he called her contribution "snooping") a murder case a few months ago and formed a grudging respect for each other.

Exactly twenty-four hours after Kate and Marlene had disembarked from the *Shady Lady*, they were sipping chocolate ice cream sodas in Dinah's, maybe the last coffee shop in America that allowed small, well-behaved pets to accompany their mistresses. Ballou sat happily at Detective Carbone's feet. Humph. Nick must be sneaking the Westie whipped cream.

"So, Detective, are you going to give us the scoop or what?" Marlene sipped her soda. "After all, we brought the bad guys in."

"Indeed you did." Carbone looked over at Kate. "According to Mike Hastings—that's the captain—the *Shady Lady* moonlighted several nights a month as a transport ship, smuggling Cubans into the United States. But Clive Weber got greedy, using the *Lady* to bring in drugs from Bimini. The captain, suspicious about the amount of fuel used when the boat supposedly was in port, spied on Clive. Then, together with his partners, Connie and Bob Dalton, the captain hired an actor, who did a little moonlighting himself as a hit man, to give the performance of his career."

"Killing Clive," Kate said.

"Was Clive dead in the water?" Marlene asked. "Did you find his body?"

"Yes. He washed up on Deerfield Beach an hour ago. A bullet in his brain."

Kate let out a sad, little gasp. Ballou nuzzled her ankle.

"You two, as older women, were specifically chosen to be their audience, to bear witness to Clive's murder by a crazed Cuban who, after having killed the Holiday USA host, would—as scripted—jump into the dingy and take off."

"Older women with gusto," Marlene said.

Nick Carbone smiled. "Right. And those characters never had a clue your improvisations would bring down their final curtain."

Noreen Wald, aka Nora Charles, is Secretary of the Board of Directors of Mystery Writers of America. In 2004 and 2005, she served as MWA's Executive Director. She also is the founding president of MWA's Mid-Atlantic Chapter.

As Nora Charles, she writes the Berkley Prime Crime Senior Sleuth Series, starring Kate Kennedy: Death With an Ocean View, *June 2004;* Who Killed Swami Schwartz?, *January 2005;* Death is a Bargain, *November 2005; and* Hurricane Homicide, *December 2006.*

As Noreen Wald, she has written five novels in the Berkley Prime Crime Ghostwriter Mystery series and two nonfiction books, Contestant: Success Secrets of a Game Show Veteran *and* Foxy Forever: How to be Foxy at Fifty, Sexy at Sixty, and Fabulous Forever.

A Rose by Any Other Name
by Leone Ciporin

I killed my husband on a Friday night. That gave me two more days before anyone at his office would notice he was gone. The kind of man he was, no one else would care.

It wasn't a crime of passion. My husband could drain the passion from a religious zealot. I just got tired of his constant, relentless criticism. If I cooked pasta for dinner, he'd pull out a piece and rub it with his fingers, testing it for doneness. If I bought a nice blouse, he'd peer at me over the top of his newspaper and say, "Well, Rose, at least you bought it cheap."

But the last straw was the Dennison party. The Dennisons were the most important friends we had. They knew all the right people and invitations to their parties were more valuable than tickets to a sold-out basketball game. One of my husband's two redeeming qualities was that his architectural firm did work for the Dennisons, which had netted us the invitation.

Naturally, I had to dress well, so I bought a designer gown, black, floor-length with a halter top underneath a filmy gauze jacket. The dress nipped in at the waist, showcasing my best feature, and flared at the hips, hiding the slight bulge I couldn't seem to lose. I lightly draped one hand on the banister, smiled at my husband's bald head staring up at me and strolled down the stairs, feeling like Scarlett O'Hara. He said, "You can start your diet tomorrow."

That was the moment I decided he would die.

The actual execution of my decision took several weeks, but the sacrifice of immediate gratification was more than compensated for by the pleasure of planning the operation. I anticipated every detail, every contingency in organizing my flight from the country and my assumption of a new identity. I didn't intend ever to return to the United States, but I like to do things right, so I was careful in selecting a new name. Too much incompetence already in the world—I wasn't about to add to it. I searched public records for the name and Social Security number of a deceased woman around my own age. Although I did choose one five years younger—why not reverse the aging process when you get a chance?

I'd decided to go to Costa Rica. Some friends of ours had vacationed there the previous year and raved about the scenery, the weather, everything. Since we'd never associated with criminals, I had no idea where to find someone in the United States to forge a passport, but with the Latin American drug trade, Costa Rica would have plenty of forgers eager to work for a price. I could afford to pay that price thanks to my husband's other redeeming quality—his excellent income.

Because I'd opted to run rather than pretend to be innocent, I didn't even wipe the fingerprints off the knife. I'd considered using a gun, but the knife was so much more satisfying. Watching his astonishment when he realized I intended to keep on stabbing him gave me a thrill of pleasure that he'd never given me in bed. I even left the knife next to his still-bleeding body. Save the police some time.

I'd already packed my bags and cleared out our accounts, depositing the money in an international bank under my new name, Sophie Hargreaves, so I made my flight to Costa Rica with time to spare. I smiled at the other passengers and asked the flight attendant for a second cup of coffee. They didn't know they were returning the smile of a murderer and a free woman. But my freedom had a price, with fleeing the country and all. I wasn't happy about leaving civilization, but other countries were starting to come around. We'd even seen a McDonalds the last time we were in Paris.

Our plane arrived late and the sun was up when we landed. Once I'd gone through Costa Rican Customs, which basically consisted of "hello," I walked outside into thick, humid air and headed for the line of taxis.

I found the seediest one, a beat-up red sedan with a thin, oily looking man, and told him to take me to the hotel downtown. Spanish music blared from his radio and his speech lacked good English grammar. I hated dealing with foreign taxi drivers back home. Now I would have to deal with them here, too.

I waited until we'd pulled clear of the airport to begin the conversation. "If I were to lose my passport, where is the American embassy?"

He shook his head. "Don't lose passport."

"Of course not. But if I were to lose it somehow, perhaps to some deserving person, would I need to go to the embassy to get a new one?"

"Don't lose passport." He paused. I gripped the edge of my seat to keep my hands from squeezing his stringy brown neck.

Eventually, he spoke. "Who is the 'deserving person'?"

"I don't know." I looked out the window casually and sighed. "I just don't want to be me anymore. Maybe someone else would like that chance."

He shrugged, but said nothing. I bit my lip, leaned back against the ripped seat cushion and began working out an alternate plan. We rode downtown in silence until the hotel's peeling roof appeared ahead of us.

Finally, he said, "If you like to meet a deserving person, I have a name. A friend of my brother."

"That would be great. I don't intend for anything to happen to my passport, but it would be nice to have the name of a local person if I need it."

We pulled up in front of the lopsided hotel, with its stucco front peeling away, seeming much shabbier than its ads had implied. The cab driver scribbled a name and number on the back of a receipt slip. I paid my fare, adding a generous tip. We exchanged papers. After checking into a room the size of my bedroom closet, I unfolded the slip and read the name: "Carlos Vasquez."

I left my clothes in the suitcase rather than risk contact with the furniture and walked down the street to a tiny grocery store to buy brown hair dye. I'd stand out less if I darkened my blonde hair. After my transformation, I ate dinner at a small, scruffy place down the street, using bottled water to wash down the over-spicy food. I went to sleep early.

The next morning, I walked through the narrow, noisy streets looking for a hair salon. I found a small alcove filled with babbling women. Everyone there spoke Spanish, which was beginning to irritate me, and the woman cut my hair shorter than I'd wanted. These people couldn't even cut hair right.

By the time I returned to the hotel, I figured the taxi driver had had more than enough time to alert Carlos to my call. Besides, my Friday night timing only bought me a few days to get my new identity. No point leaving a trail any longer than I had to.

I dialed the number and introduced myself to a man with a heavy Spanish accent.

"What do you want?" he asked.

"I have a passport that I'm looking to exchange for a new one. I'd pay you well for your trouble."

"Why don't you want your passport?"

"Let's just say it wouldn't be very useful in the United States anymore. I'll pay your usual rate for a new passport. Consider the old passport a bonus."

"Usual rate?"

I named a sum about double what my Internet research had told me passports sell for in the black market.

Leone Ciporin

He promptly arranged to meet the next morning at a restaurant a few blocks from the hotel. I arrived on time and waited. People here didn't operate on the same schedule as in the United States. I felt homesick.

I was on my third cup of a thick coffee-like sludge when a short, dark-skinned man with a stubbly beard came to my table. He smelled like sweat. "Mrs. Mallory?" When I nodded, he motioned me to follow him. "Come with me."

I followed him to a side street. He headed through a small door and led me down a dark hallway into an apartment at the back. The apartment's open windows let in sunlight and street odors. A light blue sheet covered one section of the wall. We sat down at a rickety wooden table near a tiny kitchen.

He reached out his arm. "Your passport."

I handed it over. He examined each page before setting it on the table.

"I have a name for the new passport. Sophie Hargreaves." I handed him photocopies of the birth and death certificates, which he also examined.

"We can change your passport to the new name. Or a new passport. For a higher price."

"I'll take the new passport."

"The other way would be easier."

I forced a smile. "No. The old passport is part of my past. I'm never going back to the United States and I don't want to keep anything from my old life."

He shrugged and gathered up the papers, motioning me to the far side of the room. He snapped my picture, using the light blue sheet as a background. Naturally, I asked to see the picture—I wasn't about to go through life with a hideous passport photo. Carlos stared at me as if I'd asked for the moon.

"Your picture looks fine. It looks like you."

After ten years with my husband, I knew how to respond. "I'd love to see it." Soft, gracious voice.

He continued staring blankly. But our maid was from Guatemala, so I understood how to deal with these people. You just had to repeat yourself until they got the message, which he finally did. Of course, the picture he'd taken was terrible. Those people couldn't even take a good photograph.

Again, he argued. "The picture is fine. It's just a passport."

Out came the gracious tone again. "It's a lovely picture. I just should have smiled more. Let's try it again."

The second shot wasn't much better, but apparently the best he could do. I let it go. Costa Rica was my new country and it was best to start out being generous.

Like everything else in that country, the new passport took several days, but after a brief meeting with Carlos, where I discreetly checked the picture again, I finally became Sophie Hargreaves. Next, I found a place to live, away from the noise of the city, but not so remote that I had to trek through the Amazon to get anywhere. A small house, not too expensive, but very dirty. A lot of maids back home come from these countries, and now I knew why. Cleaning American houses must seem easy compared with the dirt they have here. Travel does broaden one's perspective.

I'd planned to stay in Costa Rica permanently, but after a couple of months, the place was driving me crazy. Nobody spoke good English, they took forever to get anything done and there was no one to have lunch with. Drinking bottled water wore on me and I didn't intend to spend the rest of my life speaking the language of my maid. Besides, my husband's money wouldn't last forever and I wasn't about to work for these people.

Some time had passed since my husband's death and the story had dropped from the news. With my new identity, I'd get by if I planned properly. I couldn't go back to New England, but California would be safe. The land of fruits and nuts, as one of my bridge club friends used to say. No one we knew would ever go there.

So I headed to Los Angeles, as Sophie Hargreaves, U.S. citizen and California resident. The flight went smoothly and we landed on time at LAX. A clean airport, with people actually hurrying to get somewhere. So happy I almost cried, I even welcomed the sight of the passport official, despite his absence of a personality. For fun, I decided to get him to smile. I was single now and needed practice before going back on the market. But the man was obviously gay. I couldn't get him to respond.

He scanned my passport. "Purpose of your trip?" His facial muscles never moved, not even when he spoke.

"Pleasure. Vacation." I twitched the corners of my mouth and tilted my head. I'm not one to give up easily.

"How long were you gone?"

"Three weeks."

His large eyebrows drew together slightly and he flipped through my passport, staring at one page for several minutes. A broken clock ticked off beat. He motioned to a uniformed officer, handed him my passport and nodded in my direction.

The officer touched my elbow. "Ma'am? Please come this way."

I shrugged. "Certainly. Anything wrong?"

"Come with me." He led me to a waiting room off the Customs area and pointed to an ugly orange chair. I sat there for at least an hour, forcing myself not to run out of the room and shout at these incompetents. I didn't want to make a scene. Sophie Hargreaves had an image to maintain.

The room had an odd smell, which I soon realized was no smell at all. After months in the land of many odors, it felt strange to find them absent.

At long last, two men in dark gray suits walked in. One was tall and slender. Nice-looking, if a bit stiff. The other could've used a diet and a tailor.

The cute one spoke. "You're not really Sophie Hargreaves, are you?"

My face managed to stay calm, though my heart started pounding. "Of course I'm Sophie Hargreaves." I smiled. "Miss Hargreaves."

They sat down opposite me. The cute one said, "You've just come back from Costa Rica. How long were you there?"

"Three weeks—vacation." I smoothed my hair, making sure my hand didn't shake.

He looked down at some papers in his lap. "So, you left Los Angeles three weeks ago? What date was that?"

I cursed myself for not having checked the flight schedule. Costa Rica attitudes had obviously affected me. Looking up, I pretended to consult a calendar in my head. "Let's see. . . that would have been three weeks ago Saturday."

"From L.A.?"

I nodded.

He shuffled some papers, tilting a photograph of me and my husband toward me, before leaning forward, elbows on his knees. "Mrs. Mallory—" he emphasized the name— "your passport—excuse me, the Sophie Hargreaves passport—shows no stamp indicating that you ever entered Costa Rica. It has only one stamp showing your entry into the United States today."

I slumped down in my chair. Those people couldn't do anything right.

The idea for "A Rose by Any Other Name" came to Leone Ciporin as she waited in the airport for a Thanksgiving weekend flight. When she's not writing mystery fiction, Leone works as a public affairs manager for an insurance company. Prior to her public affairs career, Leone practiced law and considers herself a recovering attorney. A member of Sisters in Crime and Mystery Writers of America, Leone lives in Virginia.

Rear View Murder

by Carla Coupe

"Is he dead?"

Her voice broke on the last word. She pushed lank, damp hair off her forehead, the musical tinkle of her charm bracelet loud in the momentary stillness. Sunlight sparkled off the crisscrossed street signs on the corner, ghosting the words "Fourth" and "Cedar" onto her retinas.

The cop shifted his weight from one foot to the other and glanced down at her, the shade of his hat brim a dark slash across his broad sunburned cheeks.

"Looks that way." His voice an unexpected tenor. "He must of cracked his head on the pavement when he went down."

She nodded and wrapped her arms around her knees, staring at the deep scratches on the toe of the cop's left shoe. Dead. The cracked cement curb radiated heat, the thin cotton of her shorts gave little protection against the rough surface. A crumpled package of Lucky Strikes lay in the gutter beside her. His?

With a shudder, cold and hot flashing over her skin faster than a Times Square marquee, she tightened her grip on her sweaty legs. Her cotton shirt stuck to her back, drops of perspiration trickled between her breasts. It was beginning to sink in. She'd killed a man.

A muffled clang buffeted the humid air, cut off in mid-strike, then began the deep resonant tolling from St. Cyril's. They still hadn't fixed the bells, even after. . .how many years? She counted the peals. Five o'clock.

She raised her face as the sound shivered into stillness. "He just walked into the street right in front of me. I didn't even have a chance to stop."

"Yeah, miss. I got it down when you told me the first time." The cop rubbed his nose.

A local boy, she thought, her mind veering onto yet another tangent. Most of the boys she'd grown up with had noses that size and shape: squat, fleshy, eastern European noses. Over half the town could still trace its roots back to the same handful of villages on the Ukrainian-Polish border. Their ancestors—and hers—settled in these coal-rich hills, working in the mill down by the river, saving up to buy a tiny house with a deep front porch up by the Orthodox church.

Dark, wet patches spread under the cop's arms. A shrug, a glance over his shoulder at the knot of people busy on the other side of her car. "Lucky for you, you got a couple witnesses who say it was an accident, too."

Lucky, indeed.

Her lips twisted, and she lowered her head. The charms bit into the tender underside of her arm. She'd taken a man's life.

Her fingers groped for the small boot that hung on the bracelet. Drops rolled down her cheeks, collecting in the corners of her mouth. Salty, like a faint taste of the sea. The cop would take them for tears of shock or sorrow.

The door of the bar opened and three men emerged, squinting in the brutal sunlight.

Mouth suddenly dry, she took a sip of her soda and glanced at the clock on the dash. 4:07. As she suspected: creatures of habit. She tucked the cup into the holder between the seats and pulled out of the parking lot. The tires sent an empty beer can skittering across the broken asphalt. Two of the men, bellies lapping over their belts, crossed to the left side of the street near the corner. They turned and called to the other man. Brown hair scraped back into a scraggly ponytail, a faded yellow Steelers tee-shirt stretched across his narrow shoulders, he flipped them the bird and continued his shambling course down the opposite sidewalk.

Keeping the speedometer exactly on twenty-five, she headed down the street.

Not much traffic. A quiet time, school buses finished with their routes, and the evening shift at the mill already under way. Down the steep curve of the hill; remember to flip on the right turn signal and brake for the stop sign at the bottom. The two men stood on the left corner, gesturing expansively. She craned to see around them. All clear. A pause, a breath. Then she turned the wheel to the right and pressed the gas. The car shot forward.

A flash of yellow as he stepped into the path of the car.

Fast, so fast her foot still held down the pedal, the hood plowed into him. For an instant, his startled eyes met hers. Then a thud and his body rose, a crane poised for flight, quickly aborted. A shout from behind. She jammed on the brakes, her heart pounding wildly, a scream clawing its way up her throat.

He sprawled on the patched asphalt, arms and legs twisted, yellow against black. And red.

She struggled with the seatbelt catch. The belt retracted with a whirr. The two men she'd passed pounded up to the car; one wrenched open the door.

"Jesus Christ, lady! You—"

"I didn't see him!" Her nose wrinkled at his cigarette-and-beer stench. "I turned, and he stepped out in front of me."

The man raised one hand and shaded his eyes. The hair on his arms glinted gold, his fingers tightened on the door frame. The other man knelt on the street, next to the...He looked up, ran a hand over his thinning hair and shook his head slowly.

"Damn," the man beside the car murmured. "You got a cell phone, miss?"

She nodded and fumbled in the backpack on the seat next to her. Her hand shook as she pulled out the phone, and the man gently took it from her.

"We need an ambulance." His voice husky, he stared at the men in the street. "There's been an accident at the corner of Fourth and Cedar."

Her Aunt Natalie had warned her about the speed traps when she first arrived, so she'd been careful when she drove around town. Things had changed so much over the years; the neighborhood she'd grown up in suffered from what politicians called urban blight, and what her aunt called too damned high property taxes and not enough decent work. A few landmarks remained, though. Enough for her to get her bearings.

Fat raindrops polka-dotted her windshield as she turned down Fourth, passing boarded-up storefronts—the shoe repair, the beauty parlor, and the little grocery where her mother would send her to buy a forgotten dinner ingredient. Where she and her best friend Donna would spend their hard-earned dimes and nickels on licorice whips or a box of Cracker Jack. Across the street, Pete's bar, sole survivor on the block, celebrated business with lurid neon lights that could barely be seen through the grime-caked windows.

She dug into the take-out bag on the passenger seat and pulled out a french fry. Blew on it before folding it into her mouth. Hot. Salty. Greasy. So good. Scanning the deserted street, she slowed down, then pulled into the trash-strewn parking lot across from the bar.

Turning on the radio, she twisted the dial until the muted sounds of soft rock filled the car, then sat back, occasionally munching on a fry and watching raindrops spatter on the hood and windshield. Fog hazed the windows. She cranked down the one on the driver's side, clammy air thick on her skin. She'd forgotten the smell: sharp, acrid, stronger when the wind blew up the valley or when the air hung still and damp.

She'd checked her watch twice, and the fries left at the bottom of the carton were cold when the bar door opened and a man stepped out. A limp ponytail hung out the back of his black Steelers cap, jeans rode low over skinny hips. He hunched his shoulders against the drizzle and stuck his hands into his pockets before turning and walking away, swaying like a sailor newly ashore.

He staggered down the street, never pausing or turning his head, disappearing below the crest of the hill. He'd cross Cedar Street at the bottom, take the direct way home. Her clasped hands felt like blocks of ice. When she took a shaky breath and forced her hands apart, the street was long deserted. The chill in her bloodstream quickly turned to heat.

No. Hate.

She checked her watch—4:17—then twisted the key in the ignition and peeled out of the parking lot.

"It's good to see you, girl." Her aunt had smiled, faint echoes of her grandmother and mother in the shape of her aunt's jaw, in the faded blue eyes. "It's been too long."

She smiled back at her aunt and sipped her iced tea. A bead of water meandered down the glass, dampening her fingers as she stared down at the pile of potato chips and the sandwich on her paper plate. Two slices of bologna on white bread, spread crust to crust with mayo; it used to be her favorite. Could she eat it now without gagging?

"Work keeps me busy." Which was true, during the day, at least. At night, memories roamed freely. That was what she had come here for, to make her peace with those memories.

"And life in the big city." Aunt Natalie gave her a knowing look. "So, have you found a nice boy yet?"

Instead of answering, she asked about Uncle Mike and her cousins.

After lunch, they moved to the tiny living room. Aunt Natalie settled in front of the TV—a huge monstrosity housed in a cabinet, bought with pride in 1968—to watch "her story," her feet propped on a vinyl hassock, a bottle of Iron City on the TV tray beside the chair.

Time to get to work.

"I'll just make a couple of phone calls while you enjoy your show, Aunty." She had to raise her voice above the toilet paper commercial, blaring at rock concert volume.

Eyes already glued to the set, Aunt Natalie waved a careless hand in acknowledgment.

She opened the hall closet. The phone book—so meager, compared to the ones she was used to now—sat on the shelf. She pulled it out and took it, along with her cell phone, to the front porch. The big glider squeaked softly when she sat. She flipped open the phone book and slid her finger down the cheap paper, finally stopping on a name.

Still here. Still in the same house, his parents' house.

Would she recognize him after all these years? Stupid question; of course she would. She'd know him even if she turned into Helen Keller and had to run her fingers over his face.

Disgusting thought.

She knew where he'd be after work. All she needed to find out was which shift, and that should be easy enough.

It only took a moment to look up another number, pick up her phone, and dial.

"Mary Beth? Hi, it's me. Long time no see, I know. Well, I'm in town visiting my aunt, and she's in the middle of soap opera heaven. I wondered if I could come over and catch up. Find out what the old gang is up to."

Her lips stretched into a smile and she pushed back her hair.

"Great. Let me grab my purse. See you in a few minutes."

"Who's that?"

Frowning, she had stared at the guy standing across the school parking lot. He leaned against the hood of a white Camaro, his crossed arms almost obscuring the Steelers' logo on his shirt. A chill breeze tossed strands of long brown hair around his face and stirred the thick layer of leaves on the pavement.

Mary Beth pitched her books into the back seat of the green-and-rust colored Gremlin and turned, looking out over the sea of students leaving the building. "Who?"

"Over there, next to Jimmy's car. Brown hair, black shirt."

"Him?" Mary Beth squinted, too vain to wear her glasses outside. Johnny Kachmarik still hadn't asked anyone to homecoming, and she wanted to be prepared, just in case. "I don't remember his name, but he graduated six years ago with Bill. Why?"

With a shrug, she shifted her books to her other arm. "I recognize him from somewhere."

She knew where. She'd never forget that face, that car.

"Oh, yeah?" Sliding into the driver's seat, Mary Beth buckled her seat belt. "Are you coming, or what?"

She pulled her gaze from him and opened the door. "Ask Bill who he is, okay?"

"He looks like a real loser, but sure."

"I saw the car!" Her voice had caught, and a large hand had pressed on her shoulder, gently pushing her back into the bed. Every part of her body hurt, and she blinked away tears. Tears were for babies; she was eleven, a big girl. She knew what she'd seen.

"Sure, honey." The hand lifted, and the big policeman picked up the pink plastic cup with the straw and held it to her lips. "Can you describe it?"

She took a sip of water, flat and metallic on her tongue. "White." She closed her eyes, but the image stood out clear against the blackness. "With a big hood and wheels."

"And did you see the driver?"

She nodded once, even though her head ached. "A man. With brown hair."

"Okay, okay. You get some rest now."

His footsteps sounded loud on the linoleum as he crossed the room.

"Will that help find the car and driver?" Her mom's voice, a harsh whisper. When they'd wheeled her out of the ambulance and into the hospital, she saw them, her mom and her dad. Her mom had cried, big, fat drops rolling down her cheeks and dripping off her chin. Her dad had just looked sad, as he often did.

"Not really, but we'll do what we can." The policeman wasn't good at whispering. "She was damn lucky that the car didn't hit her head on, otherwise she'd be dead, too."

She didn't open her eyes, and after a while, the policeman went away.

"You'll always be my best friend." She had popped a handful of Cracker Jack into her mouth and caramel sweetness had blossomed on her tongue. She crunched the popcorn as the grocery door jangled shut behind them.

"And you're mine." Donna dug into the box. "For you." Sticky fingers pressed the little charm into her palm.

She peered at her hand. A boot. Perfect for the bracelet her mom and dad had given her for her birthday. "Thanks." She shoved it into her pocket.

A grin behind a curtain of blonde hair. "Race you home." The flash of a blue tee-shirt and coltish legs starting down Fourth.

"Hey, no fair!" She clutched the bag of potatoes her mom had asked her to get for dinner, and ran after.

At the corner, Donna glanced over her shoulder. "Come on, slowpoke!"

The car came out of nowhere.

Fast, so fast there was no time to shout, no time to even take a breath. Donna's small body hit the hood with a thud and lifted, an egret poised for flight.

"Donna!" she screamed. Then the fender struck her left hip and side, and, for an instant, her eyes met those of the man in the car: wide, startled, scared. Then she, too, was flying, but only for a heartbeat. She fell. Her skin burned as she skidded across the asphalt, her head hitting the pavement so hard she felt as if her skull had cracked open. Pain, so much pain she couldn't tell where it ended and she began, but she forced her head up, willed her eyes to focus.

Donna lay sprawled on the street, yellow hair against black. And red.

The car revved, reversed, and sped away. She stared at the sky, as blue as Donna's shirt.

Remember the car.

Remember him.

A former researcher at the Smithsonian Institution and the National Gallery of Art, Carla Coupe is a member of Sisters in Crime, and a member of the board of her local chapter of Mystery Writers of America. She fills her spare time belly dancing, gardening, and enjoying life with her husband and son.

The Last to Know
by Elizabeth Foxwell

His wife, he reflected with a patronizing sniff, was always the last to know.

Like when he had arrived home this evening to find his neat row of rosebushes had suddenly and unaccountably withered during a lush summer.

"I don't know, dear," she said with her maddeningly vague, fussy smile, when he asked about the cause.

Or when she had moved his financial records when they were perfectly aligned on his desk.

"Did I, dear? I don't recall."

The last straw was when Lorraine's long-promised legacy from Great-Aunt Bertha failed to materialize, and all his careful plans—the whirlwind courtship, the hasty marriage, and the next step, the tasteful funeral—had dissolved in frustration. Lord knows he had taken pains to assume the right roles. Outfitting the new wife—Devoted Husband. Flattering the new wife's ancient relative who had gazed unwinkingly at him out of one milky eye—Dutiful Nephew-in-Law. Practicing at the mirror for the right touch of guileless pathos—Brave But Forlorn Widower. Who knew the old bat's will, which referred to her "greatest treasure," actually meant a bossy geriatric feline named Cassie?

"Great-Aunt Bertha," said Lorraine, "must have known best."

From its perch on the serving cart, the "legacy" regarded him balefully, then jabbed a vicious paw into the delicate soufflè. It promptly deflated. He swore, and Lorraine gave Cassie a half-hearted cuff about the ears and a tidbit of something. The cat promptly threw up, to his further disgust.

"Bad kittums," she crooned, mopping up the mess. The cat purred with satisfaction, turning its furry back upon him and swishing its molting tail into his face. Lorraine picked the cat up, Cassie smirking at him from the safe cradle of her arms.

The beast would be disposed of, he promised himself, spitting out tufts of cat hair. Right after Lorraine's...well, departure. And he would procure a delightful pit bull that ate cats for breakfast.

Cheered by the thought of canine cuisine, he savored a mouthful of garlic potatoes. It really was unfortunate; Lorraine was an excellent cook. But she had to go. His investments were prospering at a satisfactory rate, but even without Great-Aunt Bertha's money, Lorraine's life insurance payoff could comfortably buy a new cook and a beach house in the Bahamas without dipping into his security or saddling him with the inconvenient baggage of a wife.

That is, if he rid himself of the wife. Because poisons or bullets were tools of far clumsier men than he, subtler stratagems were called for. Without the untidy caprice of Great-Aunt Berthas, he believed, life was orderly. There was no reason why death could not be so as well.

But his attempts had not proceeded according to his beautifully organized plan. The sawed-through basement step had not fully collapsed under Lorraine's scrawny weight, but Lorraine, as usual, was clueless.

"Now how did that happen?" she twittered, hanging like grim death onto the banister as he scowled and Cassie hissed like an angry boiler.

Nor had the library stepladder cooperated. The damn cat had yowled when he pushed the ladder, and Lorraine had grabbed the built-in shelving for support, resulting in a mere twisted ankle instead of a twisted neck. Roused by Cassie, Dr. Freitag appeared from next door and insisted on binding it. Lorraine had thanked him prettily—although the man was a psychologist and not even a proper physician, he reflected with an inward snort—and the fickle feline had bumped against his neighbor's legs like an old friend.

He considered the electrical-appliance-thrown-into-tub-of-water-with-bathing-wife scenario. Yes, that would do nicely. He could already feel the warmth of the tropical sun on his face...

The cat threw up again, this time on his handmade Italian leather loafers, spoiling his idyllic, Lorraineless dream as well as his expensive footwear. "Lorraine!"

"Oh dear," she said. "Maybe you should take those off."

Mistress of the obvious. He kicked the shoes off with an oath and she knelt to attend to the mess.

"I suppose I should take Cassie to the vet."

A wild hope surged within his breast. "To be put down?"

"Of course not, Henry. To look into her tummy trouble."

His hopes deflated. "Oh."

"Haven't you heard a word I've been saying?"

"Er . . . I've been concentrating on your delicious dinner, my dear." He was ravenous, after all—Lorraine was unaccountably slow in putting tonight's meal on the table.

"Hmmph. I think sometimes that's why you married me—to get a full-time cook."

He frowned over his plate of meatloaf and gravy—his mandated Wednesday menu. Routine was comforting, imposing order on life. That was what led him to Lorraine, who had waited on him with brisk efficiency when he breakfasted at the cafe every day for three months. She was part of the landscape. Not too bright. Predictable. No surprises there.

He prodded his vegetables. "The cauliflower is over-cooked."

Her head bent over her plate, and he contemplated her dark roots with distaste. The first Tuesday of the month she had her hair colored. She must have missed the appointment. "Lorraine, if you need money for the beauty parlor, you should ask. You know I give you everything you want." No one could call Henry T. Platt a bad provider—part of his Devoted Husband role. Those neat folders in the study held the evidence of years of careful investments.

She pushed her potatoes around the plate.

He sampled his meatloaf, chewed carefully—eight times, no more, no less—and swallowed. Not bad. Yes. A little drier than last week's—with a strange piquancy, surely—but quite tolerable.

Anger would only upset his digestion. "What is it?" he asked patiently. Really, he was a most remarkable man, with admirable composure. "Is this about working again? You don't need to work anymore. That's why you quit the cafe."

"No, I left because you ordered me to quit. I thought you were concerned about me. I didn't realize that you were looking for a full-time waitress, nanny—and patsy."

He would not fight; there were still three potatoes left on his plate.

"You never go anywhere, and keep me here. I can't even have friends over. I'm like a prisoner. Well, no more."

He continued eating and speaking deliberately. "I hope this is not a conversation about divorce, Lorraine. You will recall the prenuptial agreement." That had been his idea to safeguard his Bermuda funds.

"Vividly." Her face bore a small, self-satisfied smile, like the cat. He stopped chewing.

"What?"

"Didn't the meatloaf taste different tonight?"

He recalled the strange piquancy. With a strangled gasp, he broke for the phone and called police. A burly young officer appeared promptly along with Dr. Freitag.

"What's the problem?"

"She's—she's trying to kill me!"

The official eyebrows shot skywards, and Lorraine came in. He saw with horror that her hair was a radiant blonde, with no trace of dark roots. His mind reeled. "What happened to your hair?"

She glanced at the officer, her eyebrows matching his in height. "Dyed it. You remember, Henry. The first Tuesday of every month is my hair appointment."

"She must've been wearing a wig. There was something in the meatloaf," he babbled at the policeman. "She experimented on my rosebushes first, then Cassie next."

The official forehead wrinkled. "Sir?"

"My roses died. Here, I'll show you." He headed for the porch door, and stopped. The rosebushes stood upright, healthy, their soft heads waving in the breeze.

"As you can see, officer," said Lorraine, in a perfect imitation of his previously calm voice, "the roses are fine."

The officer nodded and spoke into his walkie talkie.

"They were dead! And what about Cassie?" he cried. "The cat suddenly getting sick? I tell you, she tried the poison on it first!"

Cassie appeared and rubbed against the policeman's leg. Its rumbling, healthy, traitorous purr could be heard a block away.

An ambulance arrived, and the two attendants strapped him, struggling, to a gurney. Lorraine hung on the arm of Dr. Freitag, who murmured medically about "overwork" and "a good long rest"—and put one earthstained athletic shoe behind his immaculate khakis. No wonder dinner had been delayed. Henry pictured his suntanned wife with the psychologist on a Bahamanian beach, courtesy of the line of fat folders in his study.

And he wondered if an analysis of the meatloaf would reveal not arsenic or strychnine, but innocuous chili powder.

He saw Dr. Freitag's solicitous hand move from his wife's shoulder to a more comfortable position on her rump.

As the ambulance door shut with finality, he thought how this time he had been the last to know.

Elizabeth Foxwell has published nine short stories. Her short story set in World War I "No Man's Land" won the Agatha Award and was nominated for a Macavity Award. It appears in World's Finest Mystery and Crime Stories *(Tor, 2004) and* Blood on Their Hands *(Berkley, 2003). She edited the Malice Domestic serial novel* The Sunken Sailor *(Berkley, 2004) and coauthored* The Robert B. Parker Companion *(Berkley, 2005). Foxwell is managing editor of* CLUES: A Journal of Detection, *the only U.S. scholarly journal on mystery and detective fiction, and hosts a weekly radio program, "It's a Mystery," on WEBR in Fairfax, Virginia.*

Dying for a Clue
by Chris Freeburn

A lot of things will do a man in...women, booze, money, two bullets in the back, and trust.

Trust sent the two bullets into my back and landed me here in limbo, the place between heaven and hell, living and dead. You don't need employment here, but boredom is an issue. Limbo, for all intents and purposes, is exactly like Earth except you need no moolah to acquire goods or services of any kind. But the boredom factor led me to hang a shingle and carry on with my employment as a private dick for hire.

Working Shadow seemed a fitting name for an agency run by a ghost. And my name was more appropriate now than when I was alive...Callous. Of course, my parents weren't too happy with the version I took of my given name. They were partial to Calamar. Callous always seemed more fitting to me.

Boredom led me to open up shop when I arrived here two years ago and boredom made me agree to take on this case. You'd think knowing what happened when one handed out trust would have steered me clear of this man, but I needed something to do. And I was already dead.

I didn't trust Tracey Rackham's version of himself, but I found his scenario very intriguing. And I will admit, I liked the idea of spying on a bushel of dames. Tracey Rackham entered the netherworld by being drugged with sleeping pills, shoved into a dried-up well and then pummeled with bricks. Regardless of his high opinion of himself, I knew this was a man who was well hated or who knew way too much about something. And after spending time listening to him, I was leaning toward hated—beyond comprehension.

"And why didn't any of the ladies report me missing..."

Mr. Rackham rattled on while I twirled my fedora around my finger and wondered if I would get a new hat when mine was no longer in fashion. Or would it be spookier to let people decades later see exactly how a man in the fifties dressed.

"Why didn't my brother, my sister, my maid, or driver? Why didn't anyone care?"

Now, after only twenty minutes...and I had allowed my mind to wander...I had a list of fifty good reasons why I wouldn't care and I'm sure during the fifty-six years of his life, these others had gathered a list to rival Santa's naughty-and-nice list combined. The man wasn't stating his grievance with an air of dismay or a whine in his voice. His tone combined outrage, superiority, and disgust. Apparently he thought himself a man who required and should be given great devotion...while everyone else leaned toward shoving him into an early grave.

Mr. Rackham's body had been found only because a hard-working man missed the bricks he had spent two weeks' wages buying so he could add a room for his mother-in-law. If not for the man's unquenchable desire to have his mother-in-law occupy a part of the house where he wouldn't have to see her, and his lack of means to buy more bricks, Mr. Rackham's remains would still be buried under the last little pig's house.

"Well, Tracey," I began, placing my fedora on my head and tipping it back so I could catch his reactions, "the fact that those individuals didn't find your disappearance disturbing or worth looking into gives me a list of suspects to start with."

"My brother," Tracey said calmly. "I bet it was him. He couldn't believe that I would finally get married. That would mean that my will would change and that whomever I chose for my wife would be my heir and not him."

"You were choosing a wife?"

"That was what I was doing that night. I listed all the eligible ladies I took a liking to...the well-bred, attractive ones in their childbearing years...and invited them over that night to see which one would have the privilege of becoming my wife."

The man might have had money and book intelligence, but he had as much common sense as a mutt driving a car. Even with my limited knowledge of the true working of dames' minds, I knew better than to tell a roomful of them that the best woman wins me. Take a note: That is a disaster in the making. Well, with not that many zeroes past the dollar sign in my bankbook I'd get more laughs than contenders. But when you had enough money to buy any politician, it was a bad mistake to declare hunting season open on you. Which is exactly what Tracey Rackham did. He painted a bull's-eye right across his chest. It would sit better with the losers to have him dead than with another woman. No dame likes to get tossed aside.

"How many women did you invite? And why do you think your brother did you in?"

Tracey seemed like the kind of man who needed direct questions. He wasn't forthcoming on his own.

"Five," he said. "I thought that would give me enough choices, but not overwhelm me with the mundane."

I pressed my lips together to keep them from flapping open and forming words. How could any man consider a woman, any woman, mundane? I've always found something intriguing and luscious about every one of them.

Of course, that's why I wasn't killed by one of the fairer sex. Though I'm sure a few thought about it, dreamed about, and even smiled at the vision of putting a knife into me, I don't think I ever made it worth any dame's while to kill me.

"And your brother?" I asked, trying to forget the notion that whoever did him in probably did many people a favor. Take a note: I wasn't in any position to judge.

"My brother has always known that for him to succeed me, I'd have to be dead."

Good thing for him I didn't have to like a client to take a case. My main criteria is having nothing better to do.

He took my silence as assent to his superiority. "Randall was the next in line to receive the family money. Being the firstborn son, I inherited the money when our parents died."

"And after their demise you turned into one of the top-rated bachelors," I said.

He waved off my words like an aggravating fly. "Of course not. Women had always sought me, and with all my choices I had no desire to settle down. It was much better to continue tasting all the lovely treats."

"But with the deaths of your parents you decided it was time to tie the knot. Are your siblings married?"

"My brother never had the looks, intelligence, or money to have a nice choice of females to become his wife. So, wisely, he has declined entering into matrimony."

"And your sister?"

"Baby sister Claudia hasn't had the good fortune of having a proper man ask for her hand. The men she has consorted with are more interested in her taking care of them. And now with our parents gone...well, she will more than likely become a spinster."

"And why is that?" Was his sister a hideous creature? Had she shared her favors unwisely and made marriage impossible?

"Father and mother always indulged her. She lived in the family home until recently and was financed by father's hard work rather than her own. But I put a stop to that."

"How did you do that?"

"After their passing, I exercised my rightful claim as owner of the family home and gave her a month's notice to find a new place to live. And told her she'd get no more allowance now that the till was in my name. At forty, she was old enough to take care of herself."

"Did your brother have the opportunity to kill you?"

"You see, Callous, I'm having the same problem as the police. Everyone at the party knows only two people had access to the drinks—the bartenders."

"That's an easy problem to solve. You must have put your drink down or asked your brother to collect a cocktail for you. On his way to deliver it, he added an extra ingredient."

"That would make perfect sense, except I only got my drinks from the bartenders and if anyone put a glass down and wandered off, the staff was instructed to dispose of it. I knew poisoning could occur, so I tried to limit my risk."

"You thought someone was out to kill you?"

Tracey laughed. "Of course not. But knowing what marrying me could mean to a woman, I wanted to make sure none of them tried to harm each other."

"And the only one with the motive to want you dead before marriage was your brother—the only one with no real opportunity. That's quite a dilemma you have there."

"And then there's the whole issue with Madeline. But I don't really believe she killed me."

"What issue?" I asked. In this business you need all the information out in the open to come up with the true answers. Theories don't help bring a murderer to justice; they just allow someone a chance to tamper with more drinks.

"I vaguely remember Madeline leading me outside to the gardens, but I was under the influence at the time, so I could be remembering it wrong."

"Did anyone else report this?"

"Perhaps, but since my brother was the first to do so, I believe he is hiding something."

"Of course he would tell the police that if it's what he saw. He can't be too dumb to realize he'd be the most likely suspect."

"Touché," Tracey pronounced.

"And Madeline could very well have killed you to stop another woman from becoming your wife."

"But then she wouldn't accomplish her goal of becoming my wife, because I would be dead. And she knew I was very close to choosing her. With me dead, she gained nothing."

Take a note: Complications—every case had them. Tracey's brother had motive, but had no access to the means to drug. Madeline led Tracey into the garden, but had no motive. Of course, the brother, watching Madeline and Tracey, had the perfect opportunity without looking as guilty. The sticking point was the sleeping aid. How did Randall do it—or who did it for him?

"I plan to visit Madeline and investigate whether she was thinking romantic or murderous thoughts when she led you into the garden," I said. "I also need to discover if your brother could have doctored the liquor even though he didn't bring or make your drink."

"Good," he said, glancing at his watch to check on the time that no longer pertained to us. "I would like to wrap this up quickly and move forward. I'm sure there are many waiting for me in the next world."

To stick you in the rear with a pitchfork.

"Who do you think we should visit first?" I asked.

His eyes opened wide in shock and then he laughed at my naiveté about his station of life. "Why the police have them all at the house."

"Really?" That wasn't what I would consider a by-the-book move for the police. Why rustle all the suspects into one house to question them? That gave them time to get their stories straight and clean up any remaining evidence.

"Yes, everyone had returned to the house once they learned of my demise, to console each other."

I'm sure it was more like an impromptu party hosted by his brother, Randall, the new heir to a fortune and most sought after bachelor. Or a chance for everyone to get their stories straight.

Tracey and I arrived in his home to find a roaring party under way. The champagne flowed. A wide variety of expensive-looking foods covered tables in the main room. I saw a young officer sitting at the end of one table enjoying not only a leisurely meal, but also the attentions of a lovely, young, and flirtatious woman. She batted her eyelashes and looked at him with a hint of innocence in her gaze.

Was this young lady—by my calculations too young to have been a proper choice for Tracey Rackham—romantically interested in the man in uniform or trying to distract him from investigating a murder?

There was only one way to tell. Listen carefully.

"There's Madeline," Tracey said, pointing at the blonde. He sounded confused and shocked that she was flirting with the young officer so soon after his death. "I'm going to show myself to her."

His anger told me that he was starting to doubt the trust he'd placed in Madeline's innocence.

I glared at him. "Keep quiet," I said in a low voice. "Women can be very delicate and you do not want to cause a condition that results in their death."

"I don't see that as a reason to not show myself."

"It's your eternity. If you want a direct road to hell, by all means." I gestured toward the floor.

"Oh, all right," Tracey said with resignation.

I motioned for him to follow me closely but avoid brushing against anyone. Unexpected chills put people on edge and got their defenses up. And defenses can allow the guilty to walk around a trap rather than stumble into it. Most wouldn't attribute their uneasiness to a ghost being in the same room as them but to their consciences.

"Why do we have to be questioned here?" the young dame asked innocently. She started slowly moving her hips to and fro. An untrained eye would believe this an ingrained habit, but I could see it for what it was—a way to distract, tempt, and coerce information out of the officer.

He smiled at her, his eyes traveling from the hypnotic movement to her face. He shrugged. "The sergeant heard about the wake and decided it saved manpower and time to conduct questioning here."

"Does he think someone here did it?" She batted her pale lashes.

The officer, who was apparently better at his job than I gave him credit for, responded with undisguised sarcasm. "Of course not ma'am. There is no reason to think that someone here was the one to fill Mr. Rackham's glass of scotch with sleeping powder, then lead him outside so he could fall down a well, and then drop bricks on his head to make sure he wouldn't climb out. Not a reason to suspect anyone here." He gave her an appreciative look and a large grin.

She tossed her pale locks over her shoulder and stomped away on her delicate heels. The officer shrugged and returned his attention to his plate of food.

"It appears that either they don't know Madeline led you outside, or the officer doesn't want Madeline to know he knows."

"So they are trying to trip her up by not revealing what they know. Their plan is to wait around and see if their presence cracks her." Tracey rubbed his hands together.

"Either that or they want to see if she accidentally slips up in a conversation and puts herself at the well at the time of your death. It's hard to accuse someone of trying to frame you when the words come from your own mouth."

"Should we follow her?"

"No," I said. "Since she is trying to weasel information out of people, we already know she is trying to cover some tracks. What we need to know is how your drink got poisoned."

"And the way to discover that is to check on the bar."

"Exactly. Maybe the bartenders were careless about keeping people away from the bottles of booze. Or maybe they allowed someone to make their own drink—which turned out to be your drink."

Tracey frowned, but didn't comment. The very idea that people would disregard his instructions was obviously bugging him. One of the hardest things about dying was finding out exactly how much everyone thought of you. Take a note: How much—or how little.

"Why would they want to kill me?" he asked, voice laced with confusion. "What would they have to gain?"

I didn't tell him that while most murders occurred so someone could gain something, some people's personalities alone were enough reason for homicide. Like Tracey's.

"We'll just have to find out," I said. I suspected Madeline had the same mission we did. She was now trying to flirt her way into the bartender's good graces.

"What do you have behind there?" she asked, leaning over the wooden counter of the living room bar. Her movements allowed the bartender a nice look at the round, firm, lush mounds that her blouse should have done a better job of covering up.

"Liquor," he responded, pouring a drink as he tried to get a better look at the treasures offered for his view.

She stood and looked him in the eyes. She leaned closer to him and whispered into his ear, "You aren't seeing anyone? I don't want to give anyone the wrong idea. I noticed that Kelly seemed awfully interested in you."

He put down the drink he had just poured and the bottle. Apparently, interest in his job had just left his brain. I couldn't blame him.

"No," he said, leaning one elbow on the counter. "That's my cousin."

"Really"

Madeline smiled daintily at the bartender and batted her lashes. She lightly trailed her finger from his wrist to his elbow. "I'm sure glad you told me that. Maybe I could catch a ride back to my house with you."

"Sure." He grinned.

"But I may have to leave soon." She pouted her pretty lips and massaged her forehead.

"Sorry. I have to stay here until this shindig winds down."

"Well," she drew out the word, "you don't by chance have an aspirin or something like that back there?" She leaned over more to get a better view, putting her head closer to his nether regions.

With a look around the room and then a traveling glance over her rounded tush, he cleared his throat to get her attention. Instead of pushing herself back into a standing position, she tilted her head so she could look up at him.

"Um, ma'am, you're going to get hurt, and if you have a headache you might want to ask the host if he has any headache remedies. All I have back here is alcohol."

"Are you sure?" she asked, straightening her body but not bothering to readjust her skirt or her blouse.

"Yes."

"I'm sure Randall had told me he kept some back there. Can I just get a little peek?"

"No." The bartender's attitude turned from interest to annoyance. The persistent blonde wasn't winning herself the fellow or any information.

She flashed him a smile and widened her blue eyes to give herself an air of denseness and perkiness. "I'll tell Randy he was mistaken." She smiled and walked away, swiveling her hips enticingly. Though the bartender wasn't enticed in the least, his face showed suspicion and fear.

"What did she want?" a lovely brunette asked, leaning up against the counter in an I'm-familiar-with-you but not a come-hither way.

"She said aspirin, but I'm not buying it. She was just too..."

"Single-minded about it."

"Yeah. And too willing to give me a view of all her assets for an aspirin. I'm worried, Kelly. That blonde is up to something."

Kelly crossed her arms. "I saw her coming on to the cop earlier. I just got done telling the sergeant that Madeline left with Tracey to go outside. And other people remembered that too."

The bartender stared hard at Madeline's back. "You think she knows the police know that?"

"Without a doubt, Paul," Kelly said. "Otherwise why would she be trying to get information? Which is exactly what showing all that cleavage was about."

"I have a feeling we could be in a lot of trouble," Paul said.

"Either she's snooping out of morbid curiosity or she's trying to save her skinny butt," Kelly said. "Someone pushed Tracey into the well and pelted him with bricks. And that person is the only one besides us who knows they didn't drug him."

"Why would Madeline need to find out who shoved him if she's the one who did it?" Paul asked.

"I don't think she's trying to find out who did—just who she can point the finger at."

"But we weren't trying to kill him," Paul whispered.

"Who's going to believe we only doped him so I could make him take advantage of me and have someone find us so Tracey'd have to marry me?"

Tracey let out a gasp of outrage. Kelly looked over her shoulder quickly. Her gaze scattered back and forth but she didn't notice anyone. "We have to get out of here."

"Won't that look suspicious?" Paul dried his hands on a towel.

"We need to follow Madeline. If anyone gets set up with her evidence, I want it to be her."

I couldn't help but smile. The story behind Tracey's demise was getting more interesting—and so were the antics of the parties involved. I'd need more than two hands to unravel all this yarn. My best bet was to observe, aka follow, Paul and Kelly. They, more than anyone, needed to uncover the pusher and thrower. Because if not, the people most likely to be suspected of pushing Tracey Rackham and throwing bricks on him would be the ones who did the drugging.

Paul and Kelly followed Madeline into the garden and toward the well. I hoped they weren't planning to push her because then I'd have no choice but to reveal myself to stop them. I never like it when I'm forced into action.

"Why are we following her?" Paul asked.

"Because," Kelly answered, "that witch is either trying to plant some evidence that points to us or hide whatever points to her. You saw how she was coming on to that cop. She was trying to figure out what they were looking for so she could make sure they don't find it—or find something else that would make us look guilty."

"I can't believe she would do that. It's pretty low to set someone up like that."

Kelly hit him in the arm. "I think if her conscience is okay with killing, tampering with a police investigation won't make it hard for her to sleep."

"I'm surprised she hasn't heard you yet," I muttered.

"Did you hear that?" Paul grabbed Kelly's arm and made her stop.

"Hear what?"

"That?"

Her nose wrinkled up as she strained to hear something. "I don't hear anything."

"I thought I heard someone."

Kelly sighed so heavily her bosom rose and fell like a freighter on a stormy sea. "You heard me. I'm right in front of you, telling you to stop." She pointed out toward where Madeline was crawling on the ground beside the well. "What did I tell you?"

"We should stop her from planting evidence," Paul said.

"Yes, we should." Kelly's voice hardened and she flexed her hands in a manner that reminded me of a cat whose owner was about to plunk it into a tub of water for a bath.

"One of us should watch her while the other gets the officer."

"You go get him, Paul."

I watched him open his mouth to argue and then decided it wasn't worth the time. He knew he would lose. And he was thinking it might be nice to come back and see the two ladies wrestling on the ground.

At least that was what I was thinking.

A few minutes after Paul left, Kelly decided it was showtime. Waiting for the officer apparently was taking too long—giving Madeline too much of an opportunity to mess up Kelly's life and send Kelly to prison.

"I don't think so," Kelly said, coming out of the shadows and into Madeline's view.

Madeline looked up briefly and then returned her gaze to the ground. She was feeling around the perimeter of the well, her hands making squishing sounds in the damp earth. "I do think so. The answer to Tracey's death is around here somewhere."

"I know what you are doing and I won't stand here and watch you do it."

Though I noticed that Kelly didn't actually do anything.

"Then maybe your friend will help." She motioned with a crook of a little index finger for someone to come and do her bidding. "Come on and help me look."

"Paul, I thought you went..." Kelly's voice stopped dead.

I looked behind me too and there was no Paul. Who was Madeline talking about?

"Paul isn't here."

Madeline sighed. "Hopefully he'll come back with the officer soon, but I meant the guy with the fedora."

Take a note: She meant me. I decided to help her and gave myself a misty physical form. Some people could see ghosts even when we are incognito, some see us when we consciously give ourselves forms, and some never see us at all.

Kelly went pale. Apparently seeing the trees through my body—and Tracey standing beside me—let her know I wasn't with the cops. Nor could I be anyone's friend. Well, not anyone alive.

"Oh my God! Tracey!" Kelly's knees buckled and she crashed onto the ground in a sitting position.

"He is Tracey, but I'm not God. Callous is the name."

"So you are both ghosts," Madeline said. Her eyes locked onto mine. She gave me a shy smile but her eyes spoke of her interest in me. "That is so charming."

"There are more charming things about me," I said.

"I bet there are," Madeline turned her smile up to its full wattage.

"I can't believe you would kill me, Madeline. And to think I was going to marry you," Tracey said.

Madeline grimaced. Kelly gasped and jumped up. "You were going to marry her! Why she is...she is...young." Kelly finally decided to finish her sentence with that, and then turned her wrath on Madeline. "And you're trying to set me and Paul up as the murderers. How dare you!"

"I didn't kill Tracey."

"But he just said you did," Kelly motioned toward Tracey. "And if anyone would know who killed them it would be the person that got killed." Kelly finished her statement with a quick, decisive nod of her head.

Chris Freeburn

"You have to admit Madeline, Kelly does have a point," I said, shrugging my shoulders slowly so they made a smooth, seamless, eerie motion. Take a note: It didn't faze anyone.

"But why would I kill him?" Madeline asked. "I kinda hoped he wouldn't choose me." She smiled at Tracey. "No hard feelings."

"I'm dead now," Tracey said. "I don't think I can have any."

Madeline grinned.

"So you didn't want to marry Tracey. And if you knew Tracey was going to ask for your hand then that would be a good reason to kill him." It was my turn to give Tracey an apologetic look. He rolled his eyes in their sockets and waved away my lack of sincere concern.

"I wouldn't personally kill him. Too messy and I really don't want to be stuck in a women's prison."

"I believe her," Kelly said.

"Well I don't," Tracey declared. "There has to be some reason you're trying so hard to find the murderer. And even though you say you wouldn't personally kill me, you don't seem bothered that someone did."

"Tracey has some valid arguments," I said, hoping I could wrap this case up. These people were starting to get on my soul. Not a shred of real remorse in any of them—just indignation that they might be charged with a murder that they didn't "personally" do.

Madeline sighed. "Here's the problem. I did lead Tracy out here to the garden, but not to kill him. He was drunk. I thought if I took him away from the party I could claim he took advantage of me and my parents wouldn't make me marry him. It would be the word of an innocent girl against a drunk, middle-aged man." Tracey flinched at being described as middle-aged. "My parents wanted me to marry him even though I really didn't want to. My dad's business is nearing bankruptcy and this marriage could save it."

"So you were trying to put Tracey in a compromising situation so you didn't have to marry him?" I asked.

"Yep. You see, regardless of how it would help my dad, the suspicion that Tracey disrespected me and tried to soil my reputation before marriage would end the deal. My mother wouldn't have me married to that kind of man. She wouldn't want a groper in our family tree. And I did think that if he happened to fall into the well when he traveled back to the house by himself that wouldn't be my fault. And then when I heard that he was drugged, I knew the best way to save myself was to find out who added the sleeping pills to his drink. And since only the bartenders touched the alcohol..."

"It would be our fault." Kelly glared at her and took a fighting step forward. "You were trying to shift the blame to us."

"So," I stated moving my form between them, "if you didn't kill him," I pointed at Madeline, "and you and Paul didn't," I pointed at Kelly, "that means there is a third party involved."

"I wasn't trying to shift the blame. I was trying to find the killer, or killers. How was I to know that you didn't personally murder him either?" Madeline asked, with sincerity. The only real sincerity I had seen all night.

"You're right. Paul and I only drugged his drink so I could make him take advantage of me and force him to marry me. And you led him to the garden so you could claim he took advantage of you so you didn't have to marry him."

Madeline smiled. "Correct. Now we just need to find out who shoved him down the well and threw the bricks on top of him. The only people who would care if Tracey got married would be Randall and Claudia."

"It would be stupid for them to kill him, since they'd be the first ones people would suspect," Kelly said.

"It would be except that you and Madeline gave them two other people to suspect," I said. "Or at least you did the dirty work for them. They didn't drug Tracey. They didn't lead him outside hoping he'd fall in the well."

Kelly snapped her fingers. "What if Tracey fell into the well all by himself and broke his neck, then Randall and Claudia came along and tossed the bricks on top of him? That wouldn't make them guilty of murder. Just trying to give him a cheap burial."

"But that doesn't make sense," I said. "What would they gain if Tracey went missing? If he died by accident, in a drunken fall, they'd get all the money with no worries about pesky police investigations. The coroner could easily figure out that Tracey died from a broken neck." I was on my way to closing this case and helping Tracey's soul reach its final destination. "And they wouldn't be responsible. They didn't drug his drink, and everyone saw Madeline take him outside," I said, pointing out the flaws in their theories.

"But what if I wasn't dead?" Tracey asked. "What if I was injured?"

"If only we can find out who took the bricks," Kelly said.

"You don't need to find out anything." Another voice entered the conversation. The young police officer Madeline had flirted with was leading a confused, handcuffed Paul toward us. Five officers brought up the rear with Randall and Claudia, also in handcuffs.

Kelly's and Madeline's mouths fell open.

The officer pointed to the two women. "Cuff them."

They both started to argue, but the officer cut off their words. "You see, police do this weird thing called fingerprinting. That's how we learned that Randall's and Claudia's prints were on the bricks. Which of course they shouldn't have been, since neither of them had volunteered to help the owner of the bricks build his addition. And besides Tracey's prints, the only other set on the poisoned glass was Paul's." He grinned at Paul. "And being the great guy he is, Paul filled us in on the rest of the plotting in this murder. Now of course, Paul says he and Kelly only drugged Tracey. And that Madeline only led Tracey outside hoping he'd fall in the well. And when they found Tracey had somehow gotten himself stuck at the bottom of a well, Randall and Claudia only tried to ease their dying brother's suffering by throwing bricks on him."

"So you're going to charge us all with murder?" one of the quintet demanded.

The young officer shrugged. "Hey, I'm just booking you all. I'll let the District Attorney sort it out. I'm glad I decided not to go to law school. I sure as heck wouldn't want to try this mess."

Take a note: Sometimes you are damned if you do and damned if you try.

Chris Freeburn is the author of Parental Source *and* Generation Without Souls, *police procedurals that also focus on the social elements of law enforcement and crime. Her recent novel,* Dying for Redemption, *features Callous Demar, a private investigator whose ghostly existence causes his agency to move from earth to limbo. Chris is a former JAG Army specialist and spent many years as a paralegal in the Commonwealth of Virginia. She is a member of the Chesapeake Chapter of Sisters in Crime and the Mid-Atlantic Chapter of Mystery Writers of America.*

Murder at Sleuthfest
by Barb Goffman

Mother was always vigilant about hygiene. Someone sneezes near you, wash your hands. Leave the house and touch anything, wash your hands. And don't just wash them, scrub them. When I got older and started wearing rings, Mother trained me to remove them when I washed. Mustn't let germs hide beneath the band.

Even now, with the advent of Purell and Mother dead a good twenty-five years, I'd wash my hands thirty times a day if I could. I might not have noticed the effects of the disease so early if I weren't meticulous. The slight tremor in my fingers might have escaped me five years ago if I hadn't paid so much attention when I scrubbed.

I'd never have known back then that the disease that killed Mother had come for me too.

Three kids in my family, but I'm the one who watched her die. My brother, Dave, is a Manhattan shrink. When we realized Mother was becoming helpless, he had a kid and an extravagant wife to support. No way he could afford a sabbatical from work. Marion, my little sis, was in law school. We told her not to take time away from school. She happily obliged. Mother had imposed a fear of germs on Marion, too. So much so that when Mother got the disease, Marion shied away, even though it's not catching.

That left me. The unmarried mystery writer. I could practice my craft from anywhere, and I had nobody to leave behind. So I packed up and moved back home to Philly. To Mother's sterile house. And I watched the disease attack her muscles, destroying her mobility and, in turn, her dignity. Until the day she couldn't swallow anymore. She refused a feeding tube. We buried her two weeks later.

The doctors told us the disease wasn't hereditary. They didn't know the cause, but they knew that.

I didn't believe them.

After noticing my first symptom, I felt vindicated, in a sick sort of way. The doctors treated me like a hypochondriac when I showed up and claimed the rare disease as my own. Now that I can't type my stories anymore, that I can't wash anymore, that I can hardly move and have to recite this in my wobbly voice, now they believe me.

But I knew from that first tremor. And I knew I didn't want to die like Mother did.

So I hatched a plan and in March headed off to the annual Sleuthfest mystery conference in Fort Lauderdale. I met up with old pals, and over a round of margaritas, I pitched my next book. It'd involve a murder for hire. I wanted to make it authentic. Who could I speak with for details? They shared names of cops. But I wanted someone on the inside, I said. My friend Gabby came through. Her town had a big case like that a few years back. She recalled the killer's name and where he sat on death row.

I sent a letter of introduction the next morning. It didn't take long for the guy to agree to see me. Guess he wanted company. Securing official permission to visit him took longer. Finally, I got it. By my third visit we were old chums. That's when I revealed my plan. I needed someone in his line of work. Could he help me?

I know I would've saved a lot of time and trouble if I'd just killed myself, but Mother had raised me to be squeamish. I simply couldn't.

It was the next February when I finally struck the deal with Rex. I never knew his real name. We made all our contact using pay phones. I felt devious, like a character in my books. That made me feel better.

Rex didn't want me to see his face, and I agreed. I feared I wouldn't be able to go through with it if I spotted him, knowing what was coming. I sent him payment in cash to a post office box. We resolved it should happen not in my town or his. And then I thought of Sleuthfest. I hadn't planned to go that year. The disease had progressed steadily, and I couldn't climb stairs anymore, had trouble opening doors. Moving hurt. But it seemed the perfect place. With all those people milling about the hotel, Rex could come and go without being noticed. It'd be easy. And it had style. Murder at a mystery conference.

Rex didn't know exactly what I looked like. The photo on my books had been taken ten years and twenty pounds ago. I offered to send a current picture, but he said no. He didn't want to risk anyone he knew seeing it. Might connect him with me. The old photo on the library book would be good enough. So I told him my brown hair now had streaks of gray. I said I'd wear the gaudiest ring I owned. A big fake diamond surrounded by large imitation sapphires and rubies. It'd be on my left ring finger. He couldn't miss it.

After the first session of the conference, I headed to the ladies room. Had to wash my hands. I removed the ring while I scrubbed and forgot to put it back on. Left it sitting next to the sink.

I realized my blunder fifteen minutes later. By the time I made it back to the restroom, the ring was gone. I hoped a kind soul had found it and turned it in at the hotel's front desk. Nope. I had announcements made in each session for the rest of the day. A ring with a large diamond surrounded by sapphires and rubies was left in the women's restroom. Great sentimental value. Please return it if you found it. I even offered a $100 reward.

I prayed the thief would be smart enough not to slip it on during the conference.

No such luck.

A scream interrupted the last session that day. A woman had been found dead in the silent auction room at the end of the hall. She'd been shot at close range, her blood soiling the beige carpeting onto which she'd crumpled. She was an unpublished author, I learned. Searching for an agent. Her hair was brown and graying like mine. And there, on her left ring finger, sat my ring.

The police questioned me, being the owner of the stolen ring, but my alibi was solid. I eventually got the ring back. I don't wear it.

I never spoke with Rex again. As far as I know, the Fort Lauderdale police never solved the murder of the woman who stole my ring.

And I sit here in my wheelchair, straining to breathe, unable to move, waiting to die. After the conference, I decided this should be my punishment. My punishment for being so scared of the disease. So scared my plan might be discovered that I let a thief be murdered.

I just wish I could wash my hands one more time.

Barb Goffman, a former newspaper reporter, is an assistant general counsel of a Fortune 500 company. She lives in Herndon, Virginia. Barb has written short stories and a suspense novel about a suburban phone-sex operator trying to stop a regular caller who's turning his snuff fantasies into reality. "Murder At Sleuthfest," a 2006 Agatha Award nominee, is Barb's first published mystery work. The story was inspired by her loss of a ring at the 2004 Sleuthfest conference, but Barb promises she took no steps to track down and murder the person who found and kept her ring—though the thought did cross her mind.

Death in the Aegean
An Elizabeth Darcy Adventure
By Peggy Hanson

"What do you expect me to do about it?" The red-haired woman's voice cut across the gently rocking deck of the *Kaptan Sevket*, where we sipped Cankaya wine and basked in late-afternoon sun. White houses outlined the village of Sogut, cuddled between azure water and rocky crags behind. The woman's orange shirt clashed with the red and white Turkish flag on our mast.

Her voice clashed with our tranquility, and so did a growl from an unseen man. "I expect you to solve it, bitch!" Menace in the voice.

"And I will solve it!" The woman's voice sounded hysterical. She was starting to cry. "You bastard, you!" The voices spoke in English, but with an accent. Possibly a German accent.

Cordelia, Fran, Nancy, Erika, and Ginny all looked at me, then at Oguz, lounging with a beer. On this hand, my friends, to whom I'd promised the perfect tour of Turkey. On the other, my ex-brother-in-law and student from Peace Corps days. This wasn't language any of us used. In our day, ladies didn't even hear such things. I could tell from his face Oguz was upset that the group of what he told everyone were "high-class ladies" should be subjected to the indignity of overhearing a coarse argument.

The irritating interruption forced me into semi-journalist mode even though I was on vacation. Is this a mark of bias in the modern press that any hint of violence needs to be covered, while peace just happens? Not for the first time, I questioned my chosen profession. Maybe if we ignored the ruffians, they'd go away. Or after dinner, we could sail away on our 98-foot ketch with its six cabins and six bathrooms. Oguz had one of the bedrooms, so the rest of us drew lots each night to see which two would share one of the cabins. The lottery system for roommates meant we'd gotten pretty well-acquainted on the trip. Tonight I was sharing with Fran.

"Ahem," I said to my group. The slight shiver of tension and fear infecting us from the next boat evaporated. A tinkly laugh started with Nancy and pulled us once more firmly into a group.

The dueling pair next door had apparently gone ashore or into a cabin. We heard no more.

Oguz introduced us to Durali Bey, who had come with his own little bus to take us up the mountain to his Manzara restaurant.

All the bus windows were open. Wild thyme on the hillsides scented the air. Goat and sheep bells announced the end of a hard day grazing on the slopes. Pastures were interspersed with feathery pines. No wonder Turkish lamb is so incredibly tasty. Goat, too, though a little foreign to the Western palate.

In front of modest white houses, honest, hardworking villagers talked together, getting ready to eat, a few men wandering off to the little mosque for evening prayers in response to the solemn, plaintive call from the minaret, *"Allah...huwa akbar...."* God is great....there is no God but Allah.

By the time we'd arrived at the restaurant and met Durali's handsome family, the incident on the next boat was almost forgotten. Vacations aren't always the escapes they're meant to be. Couples sometimes erupt into arguments. Probably nothing there to worry us.

We sat in a row at the long table on the small open patio so we could all face out to sea. Directly across from us, the

Resadiye Peninsula groped rocky fingers into the Aegean inlet. To our left in the distance lay the Greek island of Simi. The headland where we sat was the beginning of the Taslica Peninsula, where Oguz has invested a lot of money to prepare for environmental development and is kind of an honorary aga. At its tip lies the ancient city of Loryma, accessible only by sea. That's where the Aegean meets the Mediterranean—a marriage made in a heaven populated by Greek and Roman gods, and probably other deities needing a heavenly residence.

The sun made its farewells over Resadiya, turning the mountains and sea first gold and then pink. Even the air seemed to flush. My camera, responding to my journalist need to record everything, clicked incessantly, both at the view and the cast of characters. As usual, Fran was our representative of chic, wearing a natural linen smock to the knees over white pants that showed off long slim legs. Seventy-five? No one would believe that. Fran's elegance transcends age.

For appetizers, we nibbled fresh calamari and delectable vegetables done in olive oil, garlic, onion, and lemon juice. Ginny tasted the food. "This is remarkable," she said. Rare praise from one who keeps herself and her views to herself. I've sometimes wondered if Ginny has a parallel life to the one in which we know her.

"It's the best calamari I've ever eaten," chimed in Nancy. You couldn't tell from the way she was devouring the food at the Manzara Restaurant that Nancy didn't like fish. Could the Nancy deep down be as nice as the one open to public view? Can anyone be that nice?

As dusk fell we began to see lights twinkle over on Simi—and the peace of our dinner was broken. Another party arrived, slightly drunk and noisy. Durali Bey seated them at a table near ours. Six pairs of schoolmarm eyes swiveled from our table to theirs. I expected someone to say "shhhhh." Probably that would be Erika, the scholar of our group, or Ginny, whose career spanned teaching and museum work. Oguz looked aghast. This restaurant was his special preserve—though of course Durali couldn't turn customers away.

In the group was the redhaired woman from the boat next to ours. She was laughing loudly now, probably high on alcohol or something else. There was another woman, and two men. A mix of Germans and Turks, to guess from their accents. Couples, maybe. At least travelling as couples. They were in their thirties or forties—mere children to our more mature eyes.

One of the men was Apollo-like. You couldn't help noticing him. Blond, trim, tanned. But when he spoke, I recognized the menacing voice we'd all noticed on the boat. This god-like male had behaved unbecomingly, at least, and threatened a woman, at worst. He seemed to be in charge of the raucous group. "We will tomorrow go to Loryma. Just be careful of snakes." Yes, he was German. We all looked at Erika, who was born in Germany and can't stand German tourists. Her ice-blue eyes appraised the intruders.

A grin curled Fran's shapely mouth. "Your version of the Ugly American," she teased Erika, who grimaced.

"Why can't they just stay home?"

The redhaired woman heard the exchange. It seemed to bring her out of her stupor. "Stupid people!" she shouted. "Stupid, stupid, stupid." She poured more from the bottle of wine on their table.

"Shut up, Sonia," said the handsome man. "Shut the hell up." He glanced at our table, where members of our group were visible in candlelight from the table and the last rays of sunset. It wasn't a friendly look. "Here, you!" he shouted at our hospitable hosts. "Raki over here for me! Now!" Raki is the drink of Turkey, strong, colorless until it turns white with water, anise-flavored. They call it "lion's milk." You have to be a lion to withstand its effects.

The spell broken, our group began to chat. "How do you think they found out about this restaurant?" Cordelia whispered to me.

Oguz overheard. "All the ships' captains know about it," he said. "And good thing, too, for Durali's business. I'm sorry it hasn't worked out so well tonight."

The woman we now knew as Sonia was beginning to droop into her plate. Everyone ignored her except the dark-haired man on her right, who pushed his chair close enough for her to lean on his shoulder. "To a better life soon!" he proclaimed with a Turkish accent, raising a glass of wine. Sonia tried to raise hers and it fell to the patio floor, shattering.

Talk about breaking a romantic atmosphere.

Our group tried not to stare impolitely, but it was hard. Adonis was the only one drinking raki, but he was pushing it back with ease. He carried on a conversation with the dark man on whose shoulder Sonia rested and the woman with sleek black hair who didn't seem to be drunk. We could hear snatches of what they were talking about: "...tomorrow night...Rhodes...Mt. Ararat..."

From the snatches we heard, I guessed they were en route to Iran, possibly via Rhodes on the other side of the Taslica Peninsula. Except for being well dressed, they evoked the hordes of hippie travellers of our youthful days who had poured from Europe across Turkey, Iran, and Afghanistan to meditate in ashrams in Madras or shoot up on the beaches of Goa.

It was getting dark and Durali lit candles. Between appetizers and entrees, there was a general exodus from our table. Fran got up to visit the ladies room, down cement stairs at the far end of the patio. Ginny wandered to the stone ledge to look over the moonlit waterways. Erika had forgotten something in the bus and went for it. Nancy moved up the hill to get a more panoramic night view with her digital camera. Cordelia, ever-curious, went to look at the kitchen.

Oguz and I sat and reminisced about my previous trips to Turkey—like the last one, when John had shaken the dust of medical academia long enough to accompany me. I suppressed a sigh. John was a mix of pleasure and irritation—no need to think of him tonight.

We got back to the table in time to see a heaping plate of perfectly sauteed red snapper and arugula salad being carried our way by Durali's teenage son. He was trying to wait on both tables at once, so he'd set the tray with drinks for the other table on a third, unoccupied, patio table. There was a bottle of red wine with three clean glasses, and a bottle of raki with its small straight glass and a pitcher of ice water.

As though by magic, when the fish arrived so did most of our group, wending their way past the table of tourists, who were signalling imperiously for wine, more wine—or, in the case of Adonis, more raki. The boy had set down our dishes and was hurrying to comply with the other table's rude demands. He bumped against Fran, who was returning from downstairs. The bottles and glasses on the tray threatened to join the wineglass shattered earlier by Sonia.

"Let me help," said Fran. She grasped the two bottles just in time. The boy was flustered, but grateful.

"Thank you." He smiled shyly as she held the bottles while he placed the glasses on the table. He'd already told us he was studying English. In helping him, Fran expressed our whole group's desire to wipe away any insult to Durali's family suffered at the hands of these barbarians.

Trying to ignore our unwelcome companions, we ate and drank our wine in decorous amounts and proceeded on to Turkish coffee in tiny cups and baked halva, a mix of ground sesame and sugar. Having picked up some tricks in the small Turkish town where I was a Peace Corps volunteer, I read the fortunes in the thick black grounds left in each cup. Cordelia would have a grandchild. Fran would perform one of her Indian dances before a sellout crowd.

Oguz could expect untold wealth. Nancy would attain great happiness and prosperity. Erika's was hard to read because she hadn't drunk the coffee down far enough. I could safely say she'd be making a long trip. Ginny would meet a mysterious man.

"Who's going to do Elizabeth's?" they all asked. But no one, including Oguz, knew how to read fortunes. I wouldn't think of doing my own even if it were socially acceptable.

Because the crowd at the other table was raising its volume and our proper group looked disapproving, Oguz went to arrange for the check from Durali. In the background, the driver of the second bus waited in shadows.

Suddenly, there was a scream from the other table. The sleek dark woman was pointing at the handsome German and covering her mouth. Drunk as they were, they all jumped to their feet. All except Sonia, who seemed to be staggering to a prone position on the patio.

The decorative German was handsome no longer. His face contorted, he fought for breath and in vain tried to say something. Poison, I thought. Somebody gave him poison. I should have studied that more when I was covering the crime beat for the *Trib* in Washington. We all stood around helplessly, watching the agony of a stranger we didn't know and didn't like. Nonetheless, our mother instincts took over and we shoved one of the drunken friends away from the man so he could have maximum room to try to breathe and vomit. It was not a pleasant experience.

Oguz had his cell phone out and was calling for help. Durali and his family automatically tried to tidy up the area. Almost as if the arriving emergency personnel were guests, I thought. Often in crises, thoughts and actions are irrelevant.

The police arrived in a force of two. The entire law-enforcement community of Sogut, I guess. They had an ambulance with them, manned by a couple of sturdy young men who gathered up the distorted form of the German and arranged him in the vehicle for the ride to the nearest clinic. The dark-haired woman jumped in with him. The siren rent the country air, probably waking a few sheep and goats, and certainly creating gossip among the villagers that would continue deep into the night.

Oguz and Durali held long discussions with the police while the rest of us stood and sat around uncomfortably. I heard Oguz telling the police, as he had the boat staff and others, what high-class women we were. "They wouldn't have anything to do with this. Please let them go back to the boat."

The police looked us over dubiously, and I found myself trying to look through their lens. Ginny, trim and firm from yoga, face never betraying her thoughts. I'd known her for six years, since a joint stint in India. I counted Ginny as a close friend, but at the same time, a very private person. What did I really know about her? I knew she was tough as nails—just ask the weeds in her garden.

Nancy, refined and gentle, eager to hear other people's stories rather than brag about her own career as a well-known book critic—a career that had brought us together many years ago as colleagues. We'd been out of touch for several years. Could Nancy's desire to talk about anyone rather than herself have roots in secrecy of some sort? Not for the first time, I thought what a perfect disguise Nancy's sunny disposition could be.

Fran, towering above us all, inscrutable and as elegant as always, was my neighbor on my first India tour nearly twenty years ago. A most reliable person. Hordes of friends. She'd never let me down. And yet, at times I'd sensed an iron will in Fran. There were unexplained incidents in her previous life. What were her limits?

Cordelia, looking as regal as her name and as majestic as the Smithsonian Institution where she works, was an old friend from previous days in Turkey. We'd been buddies for so long. And yet, another private person. One could never be sure what she was thinking. Could there be another side to Cordelia? Certainly, I'd seen flashes of anger at times. But she didn't even know those people.

Erika, blond and German in looks, but pure Oxford and Cambridge in voice and manner. A friend from the same tour of duty in India where I'd met Ginny. Wonderful hostess. Competent in the extreme. Competitive too, judging by her tennis exploits. Erika as a "fixer" might not stop at removing anything that got in her way.

I didn't count myself in the group of suspects, but probably should have from the police's point of view. Adventurous is what people often call me. Ready to jump in. Lots of international travel, so a passport full of suspicious visas. Fortunately, I had cachet here from being old friends with Oguz, who has standing in the whole Taslica area.

All in all, it was an impressive group. I loved them all as friends. I wouldn't like to have any of them as enemies.

After a little half-hearted questioning, with Oguz as translator, we were allowed to return to our floating hotel. The bus ride back to the pier would have been frightening in daylight. By night we had to go into fatalist mode, clutching our blue bead talismans against the evil eye. Durali himself drove us down, as he had up. It only took ten minutes, and we were too preoccupied with imminent mortality to gossip about the unseemly events at the restaurant.

Captain Hasan and our crew waited with large, slightly nervous smiles, and hands out to help us up the wobbly gangplank. The other boat was eerily silent. We knew the residents were up at the restaurant or at the clinic. Where was its crew? They must be aboard. No one would leave a boat like that unattended.

Captain Hasan made a comment to Oguz as he came aboard. I didn't hear it, but the two of them looked grim.

At the big wooden table on the rear deck, Nancy and Erika took out their journals to jot down details of dinner. Ginny, Cordelia and Fran were up in front, lying in the dark on the bright blue mattresses looking at the stars. I was heading up to join them when Oguz pulled me aside.

"I'm afraid we've got a little problem," he whispered.

"What?"

"Captain Hasan says the German died at the clinic."

I wasn't too surprised by the news, only at the speed with which it had made its way to our ears.

"So how's that our problem?"

"The security people are on their way from Marmaris to check into the death. They think it was poison. They want to ask us some questions."

"Tonight?" As I asked, I realized it would have to be tonight. No peaceful stargazing for us.

The security men met with us as a group around the spacious table in the main cabin. "Did any of you notice anything that might be helpful?" Oguz translated.

Erika sat in frozen silence, her wineglass forgotten in front of her. Cordelia looked horrified, apparently trying to think what to say to get the policemen to leave. Fran seemed impatient with the whole process and sipped a gin and tonic in her usual ladylike way. Ginny drank more white wine, appearing as inscrutable as always—almost amused. Nancy, who was nursing a club soda, looked like she was taking mental notes for a book, or at least a report.

So it was up to me. "We all heard the redhaired woman having an argument with the man," I volunteered. "She said she was going to solve something. They were both very angry."

This all got noted down. "But at the restaurant, did you see her get close to his glass?"

"No, but we really couldn't see the other table very well. It was dark. Just candlelight at the tables. The woman kept standing and sitting. She was very drunk. I guess she could have gone close to the glass or the bottle." I was pleased my rusty Turkish was rolling off my tongue.

Oguz looked so innocent sitting there translating for the others. Good heavens, in all the excitement, I hadn't even thought that he might have something to do with the death. The murder. Oguz has always been a man of passions. He might think that ridding the world of one crude man who polluted the peace of the Taslica Peninsula and insulted his guests would be a good deed.

"Do we know what these people are doing here?" I asked.

"Not yet. But we intend to find out. But I think we need not keep your party up later tonight. We can find you at Loryma tomorrow if we need to ask more questions."

It was my strong feeling that someone in that room was holding his or her breath. I looked around the circle again. Gentlewomen, with a couple of tan-suited police and an entrepreneur. I decided maybe a smile would ease the atmosphere.

"So do we sail tonight or not?"

Captain Hasan looked at the officials for approval and then nodded. "We can go out in the bay. We won't be disturbed out there." With brusque nods, the police left our boat. Dealing with women was bad enough. Dealing with six independent American women of a certain age was beyond the realm of duty.

As the *Kaptan Sevket* rounded the little island in the bay at Sogut and started to drop anchor, a motorboat with lights headed toward us. As it pulled up, we saw it had the man with dark hair, the one not drinking, and the girl Sonia.

"Ahoy!"

"What do you want?" asked Captain Hasan.

"Please to come aboard. Need to talk."

The 'please' was magic. Hasan and his crew lowered the set of stairs on the side of our boat and held it steady for our strange intruders.

The dark man was older than the blond German, but just as handsome. He spoke with a Turkish accent. He and Oguz sized each other up, sharing a bond as two Turks completely comfortable in western culture—and as a result, not quite trusted as full Turks by their compatriots. Hasan's young helpers pulled Sonia up to the deck, where she collapsed. "We need help," said the man. "I am with Turkish police."

Our motherly group had pulled Sonia over to the deck reclining area, where we had her lie down. Nancy ran to get a blanket. Ginny was checking her pulse. Fran said, "Give her air." Cordelia bunched up a sweatshirt to pillow her head. Erika arranged the blanket around the shivering form. Strange how our disdain vanished when we saw a human need.

"What has happened?" I was the one asking questions. Maybe Oguz felt too close to the situation.

"This woman was originally working with the man Klaus, the man who died, and the woman with him, Morgan. Then she wanted out and he wouldn't let her go. She is addict. He kept her on drugs. Klaus was taking something very, very dangerous into Iran. Plutonium, in fact. It is aboard the boat back there. I was planning to get help to stop the boat, when suddenly Klaus died."

"Would it have been hard to intercept the boat? What was stopping you?" I detected a hard note in my own voice. Something about this whole story didn't ring true.

"He was going to harm Sonia. He has her drugged even more than usual, which is why she is this way."

"Where is Morgan? The other woman."

"Morgan was with Klaus when he died. I think she is flying back to Germany with his body. She must be stopped."

"So what do you need from us?" Oguz had found his voice, and sounded suspicious and stern.

"From you we need help to contact Interpol. The man Klaus is searched for all over Europe. His real name is Hans Sturm. He is known terrorist. Was."

"But why not just tell the Marmaris police?" Oguz was indignant now.

"I know Klaus bribed some policeman here. I do not know which. I fear to tell. We do not know exactly with whom Klaus was working. We thought maybe an accomplice. Or even a boss. I want to radio to Ankara."

"Badge?" asked Oguz, belatedly.

"No badge. I work undercover."

We had to hope that was true.

"Is the message coded?" None of us knew what to believe at this point.

Fran's sweet southern voice cut through the silence, knifelike and deadly. "Yes. The message is coded. Send the message and then sail first to Rhodes and then to Marmaris."

We all stared at Fran. Delicate, stylish Fran. It took a long moment for the truth to sink in. Even the secret policeman seemed shocked.

"You know all about this. You killed that man!" Cordelia sounded amazed, not judgmental. The rest of us could only sit there in disbelief.

"The raki," said Nancy. "You put poison in the raki. . ."

"It had to be done," Fran said, at last. She looked a little regretful. "I still don't like killing, even for a good cause. But it had to be done."

I guessed we'd be losing Fran at Rhodes, where she'd take the first plane to her headquarters, wherever that was. From there she'd go back to her unassuming apartment in Bethesda. And one day, with luck, I'd learn what made Fran tick. Maybe even who hired her.

Never, never underestimate an experienced female.

Before sleeping in the cozy cabin where Fran lay peacefully on the other bunk—did the woman have no nerves?—I took out my dog-eared copy of Jane Austen's Mansfield Park. Everyone underestimated Fanny Price too.

Peggy Hanson has been a broadcaster and correspondent at the Voice of America, a Peace Corps Volunteer, and a teacher of English as a Second Language. She's lived, worked, and raised children in Turkey, Yemen, India, and Indonesia for twenty years. Currently, Peggy is marketing the first book in an international suspense series (Deadline: Yemen), *featuring Jane Austen-loving correspondent Elizabeth Darcy, and is finishing the second,* Deadline: Istanbul. *In addition to news reports and documentaries, Peggy has published travel articles on India, including one following the footsteps of Bombay's Inspector Ghote, hero of the H. R. F. Keating series.*

The Bartender
by G. M. Malliet

Nobody notices a bartender. The regulars may come in and bend your ear about their troubles and ask for advice they don't plan to take. But mostly, people have a few drinks and start talking to each other and they forget you're there, at least until they want another round.

That's how I first got the idea for this scheme—although I wasn't sure exactly what it was at the time. I just knew a seed had been planted when I overheard this woman blabbing away to her friend at Mike's bar.

They weren't *touristas,* these two, but locals, if an area as migratory as D.C. could be said to have locals. My guess was the one doing all the talking worked at some mid-level government job with the IRS or in the House, doing her part to help screw the taxpayers. In my line of work you get so you can separate the trust fund babies from the up-mobs as soon as they walk in the door—this one had come from the sticks to the Washington area about twenty years ago, at a guess, having read too many romance novels where women with low-powered jobs found fame and fortune helping some idiot get elected to Congress. They flock to the town "where destroying people is a sport," as Vince Foster said, and they think it's all going to be cocktail parties at the French embassy, but they do end up making six figures a year for doing absolutely *nada* so at least the fortune part comes true.

The total lack of originality in her outfit certainly suggested government employment (see clip file, Nancy Reagan, circa 1987). She wore her hair in some starburst arrangement that had gone out of style about the time *Charlie's Angels* went into syndication. She'd pinned a gold brooch the size of a hamster to her chest, and had clamped matching earrings resembling poker chips to her ears. I remember thinking all she needed was a jumper cable to complete the circuit to her brain. Probably forty or forty-five; already brittle.

Her friend was older, white-haired, with the air of a woman having less to prove. She didn't say much, but her friend didn't give her the opening for more than a sympathetic grunt here and there. She kept her eyes on her martini as if she could read the future in its oily surface, weaving her plastic olive spear in and out of her damp napkin ("Mike's: Serving Washington's Elite since 1986") but managing not to look bored with her companion. On her left hand she wore an emerald nearly the size of the olive in her glass.

I kept myself busy sorting silverware for the after-work crowd due in around six. These two were early, the only ones in the bar apart from a young couple at a high-top near the window who'd been nursing two beers for about an hour. Since everyone under thirty looks like a kid to me these days, I'd carded them both. Mike was very particular about things like the ABC laws. Not as particular about the wage-and-hour laws, was Mike, but that's another story.

Come to think of it, it's the same story. I wouldn't have been so interested in what this lady was saying about her house being burgled if I hadn't been making $2.13 an hour plus tips. That November I was set to clear about $21,000 for the year, even after not telling the IRS about every lousy tip I made. Anyway, that was why I found this fake-Chanel lady so interesting, going on about having been robbed the week before. Even then, I wouldn't have caught it if she hadn't had the bore's tendency to repeat herself four or five times per martini.

Basically her story was that she'd left her house one morning to walk her dog, as she did every morning and evening, and when she came back, somebody had cleaned out her place.

"Can you believe it? I take the dog for a walk like I do every morning, I come back, and someone's broken in and robbed me. They took everything, including my computer with the floppy disk still in it." (That floppy disk really seemed to bug her. She mentioned that several times. What did she think they were going to do—publish her memoirs?) "They took the printer, too; the TV, the stereo—everything—all while I'm out not fifteen minutes with Jacqueline."

Jacqueline. I pictured a poodle with a pillbox hat and a braid-trimmed jacket and I knew I wasn't far wrong. I was hoping her friend would ask her if she'd locked the door or left it unlocked—it seemed to me an important detail—but the friend just shook her head sympathetically and continued shredding her paper napkin with her toy spear. I was willing to bet Coco Chanel had just run out the door with Jackie O, leaving the place unlocked, knowing she'd be back in a few minutes, so why bother? Especially in the ritzy neighborhood I was sure she lived in—probably one of those houses facing the river, part of the new construction built to look like eighteenth-century town houses that just happened to have indoor plumbing and Corian countertops. I knew from the real estate ads those things, spreading like mold along the waterfront, sold for more than $1.2 million. Four BR/3-1/2 BA of valuables.

The cops had probably given her grief about being so dumb, but I thought it was pretty clever of the crooks, myself. A no-fuss burglary, all done while they knew at least one occupant of the house (including Jackie O, Guard Dog) was out. The chances were good she lived alone, wandering from BR to BA in her too-big house. They'd probably been keeping an eye on her, knew her routine.

She was irritating enough in her self-centered way that all my sympathy lay with the burglars.

The more so when she left a $3 tip on a $35 tab, after sucking up all the oxygen in the room for more than an hour and a half. Her friend noticed; when they left I found $5 more speared under her shredded napkin.

The story of the burglary stuck with me, although I wasn't sure why. It's not as if I were planning a break-in myself. Sure, I was feeling a little down on my luck, and I was wondering—again—how I was going to make the $795 rent that month and keep MasterCard from sending somebody out to shoot me in the kneecaps. I just thought it was pretty clever of whoever had done it, and it made me start to notice things about my adopted town.

First of all, you have to know that Alexandria, Virginia, is a town of trophies: trophy wives, trophy babies, trophy dogs. It seems to be an unwritten rule that if you have the cash to live in this quasi-historical, tourist-infested area, you also have to buy an incredibly expensive thoroughbred dog that costs more to maintain than an entire village in Bangladesh. This so you can spend your weekends parading the creature up and down the streets of Olde Towne, as they insist on spelling it. The rarer the breed, the more your chances of striking up a conversation with someone, preferably an attractive member of the opposite sex with money. This ploy harms no one and the dogs don't seem to mind, but the result is narrow brick sidewalks clogged with dogs and their yuppie owners virtually from sunup 'til sundown. The rest of the time the poor animals stay locked up, while their workaholic owners trot into D.C. every day to sue somebody.

It was an unnatural life for anything on legs, but it had never occurred to me someone might take advantage of this yuppie mating dance to case a joint for burglary. With an average ratio of one dog per household in the city, it made nearly every residence a natural target.

But what I could do with this new insight into and admiration for the criminal mind, I didn't know. I'm normally so law-abiding the sight of a speed trap makes my heart race, and I don't even own a car. Later that night, as I paid the house the lion's share of proceeds from the register; sparred with one of the waiters, whose favorite trick was shorting the bartenders their share of tips; restocked the bar—four trips up and down slippery ninteenth-century wooden steps hauling bottles from the eigthteenth-century cellar (four years as a history major so I could break my frigging neck on Mike's historic steps); and scrubbed down the bar for the next shift, I wondered where all my young dreams had gone. How had I ended up stuck in this dead-end job for ten years?

I said goodnight to Vincente and Lulu, who were busy sluicing fish parts off the kitchen floor, and took my $50 in cash tips for a walk through the now-quiet streets. I reminded myself that those two, undoubtedly in the country without benefit of green card via Mike's underground Salvadoran railroad, probably made between them half of what I made.

I slept badly that night, reliving nightmare job interviews and failed love affairs, which is why I was up much earlier than normal the next day—I usually sleep 'til ten or so on the nights I don't get home until two. I boiled some coffee on the hotplate and staggered to the attic window, kicking last night's clothing out of my path as I went. The benefit of living in less than 650 square feet is that it's a short stagger to anything.

I looked over the alley to the backs of the row houses on the next street. I lived on the cusp side of town, where yuppie creep was just beginning. My neighbors had changed to *nouveau riche* before my very eyes, their houses' shiny roofs and siding making painted ladies of what had once been slum houses. It was only a matter of time before my absentee landlord wised up, renovating my little place right out from under me.

I could see my pretty neighbor across the way through her kitchen window. I'd seen her before, of course. I'd been living there more than a year, but I'd never particularly noticed she had a dog—a real mutt, this one, all paws and drooping skin, like someone had let the air out of it. The girl herself was cute in a spunky, Meg Ryan kind of way, if you like that kind of thing, which I do. I watched as she stumbled around half asleep, rubbing her eyes. She wore a big Redskins T-shirt that she probably used as a nightgown. A pair of gray sweats several sizes too large for her spilled over the tops of her tiny white Reeboks. The dog watched patiently as she fumbled with an elaborate coffeemaker that resembled a miniature steel mill. Eventually, coffee under-way, she took a leash off a hook by the door and led him outside, slamming the door and breaking into a dainty trot while the old dog shambled manfully along behind her.

These old houses usually have keys weighing about five pounds that you have to use to get in or out, and I didn't see her use one.

I did happen to notice the time: 7:15 a.m. And I did sort of wonder if this was a routine that had been going on every day as I snored across the alleyway.

I just wondered. That's all.

I kept watching from my invisible perch and soon her neighbors emerged. A balding, middle-aged guy tumbled out his back door, hauled by a determined-looking, potbel-lied brute on stubby legs. The man pulled a key the size of a small tire iron out of his pocket to lock the door behind him.

Next came a middle-aged redhaired woman with some small, fluffy, yipping thing attached to a narrow leash. It might have been a cat, except for the yipping. The woman reminded me a bit of Coco Chanel from the night before. She didn't lock her door. I could even see she left it ajar half an inch.

I went to get some more coffee, keeping the scene in view, humming the tune to "On the Street Where You Live," and inexplicably feeling more lighthearted than I had in years.

Meg Ryan was back within ten minutes with her mutt, the both of them now high-stepping like baton twirlers. The potbellied dog got a fifteen-minute break, and the fluffy, yipping thing didn't return for a full half hour.

What were the odds this pattern never varied? From then on, I was up to greet the day with my neighbors. It became my routine for the next three weeks or so, even on the days I worked doubles at Mike's. Up before dawn to see Meg Ryan, who was always first into the breach, always quickly followed by one or another of her neighbors. Their schedules never varied by more than a few minutes.

Then one day the redhead was replaced by a bleached blonde in bleached jeans. It took me three worried days to figure out the redhead was on vacation and the woman (who walked the yippy creature for five minutes, tops) was some kind of dog sitter. The redhead was back in place by the following Monday.

That was the first realization I had that I wasn't just idly watching my neighbors like the guy with the broken leg in *Rear Window*. The relief I felt when the redhead came back told me I had plans for her—to be precise, for her VCR and stereo equipment and maybe her coffeemaker, if she had one like Meg's. I was tired of boiling coffee over a gas ring like I was starring in a bad remake of *Rawhide*. I could see other equipment—like a TV screen big enough for a Cineplex—through the door that led from the redhead's kitchen into her living room. And a handbag she always left next to her briefcase on the kitchen counter.

What was amazing was that they could, any of these people, easily have seen me spying on them, but they never looked up. They were too busy focusing on whatever people focus on that time of day—chores, work, what to wear, what to eat.

One day I decided to join them, running down the stairs and around the block to catch up with the redhead after I saw her leave with Yippy. As I followed her through the still-dark streets, the moon visible even as the sun emerged from behind the hills across the river, it became obvious she was headed for Founder's Park, about four blocks away. She was far from alone: The whole town seemed to converge on the riverside park, attached by leashes to every dog breed imaginable. People waved and smiled and stopped to chat as their dogs faced off in a friend-or-foe way.

So this was the local's social custom, this strange ritual where, from snatches of conversation I overheard, business and flirtation were being conducted in equal measure. The crowd ebbed and flowed for an hour as I watched from a park bench on the fringes, obscured by distance and the milling crowd too distracted by the occasional dogfight to notice a dogless early riser enjoying the view. I wished I'd brought a newspaper with me to hide behind, or a dog, but I didn't think it mattered. I am blessed with medium qualities (medium height and build, brown hair, brown eyes, neither ugly nor delightful to behold) that give me the invisible quality so useful to a bartender. Latecomers arrived with their dogs as others left, some in haste, late for work, the older ones lingering, probably retired and wanting to extend the human contact as long as possible.

The redhaired woman stood in a group, talking to some guy chained to a German Shepherd that looked disdainfully away as Yippy flipped around on the end of his leash, shrieking hysterically. The man had a sleek, banker-like appearance (does anyone but a banker wear a gray three-piece suit to walk a dog?) and the other natives seemed to defer to him as the chief at this potlatch. This was not a man who could disappear; his power and assurance surrounded him like a force field. The women, especially the redhead, hung on his words in a way that told me he was single.

When she finally managed to tear herself away, I stood up, yawning and stretching nonchalantly, and set off after her. Straight back home.

I had long since stopped kidding myself. I was, as Edward G. would say, casing the joint. I thought about finding out where the banker lived, but realized if I started with my neighbors, I wouldn't have to worry about carting away the big stuff; it was only a few feet from their back doors to the back of my place. I tried to plan ahead: I knew I couldn't just blunder in and wonder what to steal once I got there. And gloves: I'd need to wear gloves. I didn't own either a VCR or a stereo, just a boom box that had long since lost its boom, so those went on my shopping list. Any extras, well, I was pretty sure my colleague Roy would know all about where to sell stuff with a past. And cash—cash was always good.

It went more smoothly than I deserved, especially since I had no clue, no experience in doing what I was doing. Never before had I so appreciated the trials of the guys who did this sort of thing for a living.

I chose the redhead first because of her sloppy door-locking habits and for that handbag she always left out in plain view. Her crush on Mr. Wonderful told me she was guaranteed to stay out longer than the others. The next morning I was ready. Meg left first, then the bald guy. The redhead was running late. Five minutes passed and I started to wonder if she'd gone out of town again. But no, there she was, rushing out the door with Yippy taking the lead.

The backstairs to my apartment led into an overgrown fenced yard where someone once had tried to build a red brick patio before they ran out of bricks or interest. There was a door in the back fence that was left unlocked so the trash could be left in the alley. I propped that door open and scooted across the alley into the redhead's backyard. I stood still for a moment, eyes wide, ears quivering, making sure I was unobserved. Window curtains and blinds all around remained closed. All was quiet. I crept into the redhead's kitchen and shut the door behind me. Next to the door was an alarm system she hadn't bothered to set: READY TO ARM flashed on the digital display. Jeez. By now I was convinced these people were begging to be robbed.

There was a coffeemaker gleaming on the counter, a twin of the one Meg owned, which made me happy. Friendly neighbors, they probably ordered out of the same catalog. It turned out the redhead only had $26 in her wallet, so I decided after all to wrestle with the Cineplex-sized TV. It meant two trips between that and the VCR and coffee-maker. I nearly came to grief with the TV, skidding on a slobbery bone the size of a dinosaur femur Yippy had abandoned on the tile floor, but I made a quick recovery. She didn't have much else worth taking except the stereo, and by now I was afraid to push my luck. I made a mental note that I'd have to get a car soon. This was too much work, carting things one at a time, and I didn't dare strike again in my own neighborhood too soon.

No one saw me, I'm sure of that.

No one needed to.

I've been reading up on the history of the bloodhound, now that I have the time without the press of having to make a living. Also called sleuth-hounds or *Chiens de Saint Hubert*, the ancestor of the bloodhound appeared around the eighth century in France. There is a legend they were brought to England by William the Conqueror. Early on they were recognized for their uncanny abilities in man-tracking, used to hunt down cattle thieves and other sticky-fingered villains.

Their skills in pursuit are legendary, superior to all other breeds. It is said they can follow a scent for days and miles, refusing food when they're "hot on the trail," literally running themselves to death if allowed to by a bad handler. One thing that can deter them is a strong wind, which can disperse the human skin cells, which is what they really track, not the "blood" of their prey. Snow can throw them off too, or rain, but not by much. In the movies you sometimes see an escaped convict jumping into the river to throw the bloodhounds off the scent. This, I am assured by the experts, is nonsense. The dogs can smell the skin cells of the prey floating in the air even over a raging current and pick up the scent easily on the other shore. Nothing can stop them, short of death or a bad handler. And I—well, I was child's play.

I watched from my window the day of the coffeemaker caper—the redhead sounding the alarm, rushing over to Meg's house, Meg quickly emerging with her dog in tow. I now know that Meg's real name is Elizabeth. Officer Elizabeth Magruder of the Alexandria K-9 Corps, to be precise. The dog's name, if you really want to know, is Sherlock. I watched in court as Officer Magruder testified that, picking up my scent, the dog had led her straight to my door. A search warrant had taken care of the rest. This kind of testimony from a trained bloodhound handler, my lawyer informed me, is admissible in any court of law.

Sherlock, with his sad eyes and hangdog expression, also made a compelling witness. Sober as the judge, was Sherlock.

It's not so bad in here. I work in the kitchen, which feels familiar, and, unless there's a lockdown, I get to read pretty much all I want. I'm working on my master's degree through a correspondence course with the University of Maryland. Three-to-five seems to go pretty quickly most days. The powers that be made me a trustee once they saw I had no interest in breaking out from behind bars. The guards even have their little joke about it. They call me the Bartender.

G. M. Malliet has worked as a journalist and copywriter for national and international news publications and broadcasters. She was educated in Colorado and at Cambridge and Oxford in the U.K. She is the author of the Dead Perfect mystery series and is a founder of the Virginia Writers Association.

The Pink Sweater
by Sherriel Mattingly

I dashed into the biggest department store in the mall on my lunch break, bought panty hose for me and a plush toy for my new niece. Then, with a half hour to kill before I had to go back to my desk at Med Tech, I browsed. As I explained later to the judge, I didn't realize that was a bad idea.

I spotted the sweater from lingerie, three aisles away. It lay on the counter with a dozen others. But this one was soft and sensuous pink and it called out to me.

I sidled immediately to that counter, and snatched it from under the hand of another woman who gave me a dirty look. I pretended not to notice and read the tags. Washable, my size, $39.99 marked down from sixty dollars. It snuggled in my hands; definitely it wanted to go home with me. I knew I shouldn't buy it, I had plenty of sweaters, but I marched off to a dressing room.

I stripped off my blouse, eased the sweater over my head, then adjusted my bra higher, and gaped at myself in all three views. I was a siren, a Circe, a tramp with class. Even under green fluorescent lights, my skin glowed and my eyes sparkled. And that sweater did things to my body that I'd never seen in me before, though I'd glimpsed it on models in the swimsuit issue of *Sports Illustrated.*

I even thought I smelled some tangy scent like a wolverine in heat and I pictured myself snowbound on a white bearskin before a roaring fire.

I paid for it with plastic and headed for the doors, but the shopping bag suddenly felt thirty pounds heavier, and when I stopped to shift it to my other arm I spotted a tube of pink lipstick the exact shade of my new sweater displayed at a cosmetic counter. Before I knew what had happened, I owned the lipstick, matching blush and powder, cleanser, moisturizers, and body smoothers.

I almost got out of the department, but a crowd of old women surged into the aisle leaving me pressed against the perfume counter, where the wicked sales lady sprayed me playfully with a new fragrance named Sultry. And I knew that scent . . . the bearskin before the roaring fire, the darkly impetuous man who . . .

Four hundred and sixty-seven dollars later, I piled my purchases into my car. I don't know how I got through the rest of the day at the office. Somehow I kept seeing snow falling and feeling that bearskin beneath my fingers.

As soon as I got home, I snipped the price tags off my sweater and opened my closet to put it away. Immediately I could see that it went with my sleek black slacks and my open-backed heels. I had to show it off. I had to go out. I filled the tub with Sultry bath salts, bathed, slathered myself with Sultry body cream, fixed my face and eyes just as the cosmetic girl had shown me.

I donned silky underwear and the sleek black slacks and looked in my mirror. It was just me. My ribs sat there under my low-cut bra like a rack of meat in a grocery case. My tummy needed extra sit-ups. My legs were too thin. Where had I gotten the notion that I was a femme fatale?

The plush elephant I planned to give my niece looked up at me from the white carpet where it had tumbled when I dumped out my shopping bags. Suddenly I felt guilty. I should be visiting my sister, not going out to show off. Well waste not, want not. I'd wear the stuff over to her house.

The pink sweater went over my head like a tropical waterfall. It caressed my neck like a vampire. It tickled my arms like an inside out mink coat full of butterflies. It smoothed over my bust and midriff and I smelled that roaring fire and heard the soft sisss of snow driving against the windows.

My sister could wait.

I drove to O'Grady's and stalked in feeling like a movie starlet. Even the bouncer turned to watch me as I passed. I could feel his gaze on my back as I sat down and ordered a Perrier and fries. I sat sideways on my barstool admiring my reflection in the mirror behind the bar.

I barely got a glimpse of myself before some guy leaned over and ordered me a drink. Another asked me to dance, led me out and whirled me around twice before a third broke in. I could see the jealous glances of women seated in groups in the booths and I suddenly knew what it was like to be one of those frigidly beautiful models or the movie stars who make the cover of *People* magazine.

More drinks, which I don't remember drinking. A lobster dinner—in another restaurant with some tall stranger and a haze of cigarette smoke and the scent of wolverines and falling snow and thick bearskin fur under my palms and then I woke up in bed.

It wasn't my bed and I felt awful. Morally and physically awful, with a headache coming on. I don't do things like this. I do not walk into bars and waltz home to bed with men I just met.

I dressed and got out and called a taxi and showered at home, til the smell of cigarettes washed out of my hair. I resolved never to tell anyone what I had done. I kept my promise. Usually I discuss all my moral dilemmas with my sister, but to this day she doesn't know, and I didn't tell the judge either.

The pink sweater washed and fluff-dried like a charm, but I resolved from then on only to wear it by daylight.

The following Thursday morning it brushed right up against my hand in the closet like a cat and begged me to put it on.

How could it hurt to wear it to work?

And it didn't. I got through the morning OK except that Earlene was mad at me and accused me of goofing off and flirting with a heart valve salesman. I hadn't, but even John had stopped by my desk to tell me the latest jokes from the internet. Earlene glared at me, but I knew she was jealous because she craved John who sold more hip replacements than any of the others. I gave Earlene a superior smile and watched her long nose twitch like a frustrated rat's as I sailed out the door to lunch with John. We'd barely ordered before John's cell phone rang and he went off to deliver some emergency hip to South General leaving me to pay the bill. Next time Earlene could have him.

Feeling miffed, I went to the mall again for lunchtime entertainment. Window shopping is a cheap and inexpensive way to kill time. Right?

Wrong.

In Life is a Crock, I saw a beautiful fruit bowl with a creamy glaze and speckles like a robin's egg. It matched my kitchen. At the front of the store both clerks and the manager were reasoning with a customer who wanted to return a chipped set of mugs. I touched the smooth rim of the fruit bowl, then I slipped it into my bag and found myself humming the national anthem.

In The Kiddy Store I added a tiny bunny to the inside pocket and zipped it closed. No alarms sounded as I cleared the store. I couldn't believe my luck. Well, perhaps it was beginner's luck. My first shoplifting carried off with verve and style. I fairly promenaded down the center of the mall to strains of "The Marseillaise."

In the department store I hurried into leather goods. They had a wallet there that I'd wanted for two months, but I'd convinced myself the old one would do and that less was more. Humming my old school fight song, I picked up that wallet, then boldly added it to my collection.

Flushed with confidence, I glanced at my watch. Not bad for a half hour's work. I left, but as I went out, the alarm buzzer went off. Panicked, I froze, but the plain-clothes detectives nabbed a pair of women in overcoats and escorted them away. Feeling overcome, I slumped against the glass display window. Saved by another shoplifter.

At home that evening I lifted my finds jubilantly out. I'd done it. I felt a glow until after dinner when I undressed.

As soon as the pink sweater came off, I felt my stomach plummet with a thud. I looked at the stuff I'd taken and almost threw up. How could I have done anything so dishonest—not to say dumb? I hid the things in my closet.

But Saturday I woke up and picked up the pink sweater to put it in the wash. Why did I behave so bizarrely when I wore it? I held the sweater in front of me and looked in my full-length mirror.

Before I realized how it happened, that sweater was on with white slacks and I was in the car and parking at the mall.

Today I felt brave and cunning. Mata Hari-cunning. Spy-in-silk-brave and eager to carry out my mission to seduce the enemy general. But first I needed supplies. I hit the expensive shops, the ones I can't afford, but did I care? I had the unlimited funds of my government behind me.

Avoiding a Nazi collaborator, a girl who had a ratty nose, just like Earlene's, I picked out expensive cream-colored slacks and then a slinky little black number, just right to make the Nazi general tell me all. Miraculously neither item had one of those sensors that set off an alarm. On impulse, I picked up probably the only thing in the store that would fit my budget, a pink plastic bangle, that somehow looked classy worn with the pink sweater. I slipped the slacks and the slinky dress into my government's snappy carryall.

I smiled at the cashier and paid for the little inexpensive bangle while "The Marseillaise" played in the background.

And I was out the door. Unapprehended. Wow.

I sauntered through the mall watching for Nazis. And that's when I saw the earrings, diamond clips with rubies. They were perfect. Perfect to go with the pink sweater. Perfect too with the slinky black sheath that would convince the foreign general to tell me when the desert campaign would begin. I'd run my hand up his chest and remove his Iron Cross while his stubby thumbs ran up the side of my hair, just grazing my earlobes and the diamonds.

I entered the store and pointed out several things I liked to the clerk. She brought them out and fastened a tennis bracelet on my arm while my hand hovered over the earrings.

I heard "The Marseillaise" and "Rule, Britannia" play as I dropped the earrings into the carryall. So easy. Regretfully, I took the bracelet off, glanced at my watch. It was time to call London. I asked the clerk to hold the bracelet for me, giving her the name of a girl I'd hated in high school. Then I left.

"If you'll just come with me."

I whirled. It was the Nazi collaborator and she had an SS guard with her. The jig was up.

The girl with the nose like Earlene's flashed her badge at me.

And that's what I told the judge. I didn't mean to cry, but tears sneaked out as I explained that I'd never done this kind of thing before.

Whether it was the tears or my clean record or the fact that they'd lost the original evidence sheets, I don't know, but the judge gave me thirty days of community service and told me to get rid of the pink sweater.

That's when the social worker from community services stepped up. Obviously she'd taken too many psychiatric courses or read too many of those cure yourself codependent books. "It's a compulsion," she told the judge. "She'll need help. She'll never get that sweater off her back by herself."

So, over my objections, she followed me home and went up to my condo with me. Under her supervision I folded the pink sweater and put it in a plastic bag and together we took it downstairs and put it in the trash. Then she drove away in her little green bug.

I woke up at 5 a.m. sweating. What was wrong with me? I sat up shaking. And then I knew what I had to do. I had to rescue my sweater. I put a coat on over my pajamas and crept down the stairs. But someone was ahead of me at the trash cans. I hid at the corner of the condo and watched a woman lift out a plastic bag. She hustled into a tiny VW and by the time I reached the garbage cans I knew my pink sweater was gone.

A month later I spotted a headline in the local paper. Bank Thief Blames Pink Sweater. I glanced at the social worker's picture, with goose bumps running down my arms. *Déjà vu*. Somehow I already knew what the story would say.

A native Marylander, Sherriel Mattingly lives in Annapolis where she writes quirky mysteries and fantasy. In 1996 she cofounded the Annapolis Writers critique group. Sherriel doesn't need a gym. The county library pays her to juggle hundreds of pounds of books each week. They don't pay her to calculate what size corpse you could slide through the book drop, but she does that too.

Currently, she's at work on two books: a contemporary caper about a multiple personality who loves two different men, and an interstellar vacation to Ye Olde Earth, which lands the twenty-fourth-century heroine in a true tourist trap.

Death in Woad Blue
by Valerie O. Patterson

As was their custom, the two did not speak. Nor did they touch, the monk and Malkin. Instead, Malkin bent in front of him, her stained shift trailing in the dust, and placed the bundles of buckthorn berries she had gathered that morning on the stone lip of the doorway to the monastery's workhouse. As always, a thin coin perched on the edge of the rosemary pot by the doorway, and she folded it into her fist. Payment for the berries that would become a yellow paint to be used for the illuminated manuscripts the monks slaved over for endless days.

In late summer she could harvest even more. When ripe, buckthorn berries created a green the color of sap. In a few weeks the irises that grew along the village woods would bloom, and she'd harvest hundreds of blossoms early in the day before the laggards arose. The delicate blooms yielded a fine green pigment in the monk's hands. Knobby lichens scraped from rocks surrendered blue.

Malkin lowered her gaze, staring at the monk's hands, stained this day the color of cinnabar. Perchance Brother Robert was laboring over the Holy Mother's dress in a prayer book for a gentlewoman. A woman who could read, who dressed in silk, whose hands bore no thorn scratches, no berry stains. To such rank Malkin never even dreamed, such were the impossibilities.

And yet she did dream. Of brewing dyes as her Aunt Matilde did mead. For if she could blend the dyes herself, mayhap she could secure a livelihood when the time came. When her widowed aunt no longer needed her, when her young cousins Thaddeus, just eight, and Cecily, a mere toddler, would be old enough to earn their keep.

But now was not the time to ask.

Brother Robert seemed anxious. He shifted his feet in a way that suggested unease. The hem of his robe appeared besmirched with mud. Yet still Malkin did not look upon his countenance. She never looked upon the monk's face, at least not when he would be aware of it. In the village, on the rare days that he ventured out to talk to her aunt, the village's mead taster, about her supplies to the monastery, maybe then she would look out of the corner of her eye from a window or doorway. He appeared to her to be always serene, as monks should. He cuddled Cecily and patted Thaddeus's head. And yet Malkin wondered what earthly thoughts his needs must turn to on occasion outside the silent, studious walls of the monastery, especially in the golden light and warmth of a summer day. When his hand lingered on those young heads.

Brother Robert bent to retrieve the bundle, a trickle of sweat coursing down his temple as if from exertion. The stems of the berry bushes brushed the doorway as he trundled away.

Perhaps when the irises bloomed, perhaps when Brother Robert came again to her aunt's house, she would summon the courage to ask for his tutelage in the art of making ink.

Turning away from the monastery at the top of the hill, Malkin surveyed the fields that stretched in all directions, to the village along Wexford-on-Tyne River. Her aunt's house stood solidly at the edge, a bridge between the monastery and the villagers. That, or a toll house, for no one passed her aunt Mistress Matilde's house without stopping in for a tankard of mead.

From her vantage point, Malkin saw smoke rising from the roof. Her aunt no doubt had set water to boil for the endless chores of cooking and laundering. Along the ditch that ran behind the back of the house, between the house and the river where the pigs rooted and wallowed, she glimpsed a splash of blue.

Not reflected sky blue, but woad blue, the color of dyed cloth.

The color of Cecily's new shift, stitched by Malkin's own hand for May day.

Malkin pocketed the coin and, clutching her shift, dashed down the hill, calling out for Cecily as she ran. Thaddeus had been told to mind his sister at Mistress Alice's house while Malkin worked in the woods and her aunt in the mead shed. But what manner of distractions lay at hand for a boy of eight.

"Move, beasts," she said, slapping the backs of the sows as they milled around her in the yard, thinking she had come to feed them table scraps. "Where is that swineherd? I'll strike him, I will, that simpkin." The pigs weren't supposed to be rummaging about loose in the croft, crashing through the kitchen gardens and uprooting what vegetables they didn't trample.

Muddied, she reached the edge of the putrid ditch. All manner of foul matter oozed between her bare toes. But she put those thoughts aside. For up close the blue became fabric and the fabric a tiny body.

Sinking to her knees, Malkin reached down into the ditch itself and pulled Cecily's limp body from the mire. She laid the girl's head back and used her own dress to wipe mud from the girl's eyes and nose and mouth. Despite the ragged sound of her own breathing from running, she listened for life. Placed her face over the dirtied mouth to feel a faint exhale. None. No breath sweet as bee balm.

She uncurled one of the girl's fists. In it she clutched a crust of rye bread.

Holding Cecily's body close to her, Malkin struggled to stand. Muck sucked at her feet, her dress. The sows snuffled close, as if Cecily might be a treat.

"Get away!" Malkin wanted to kill the pigs with her own hands, but she could not. Except for her aunt's one spotted sow, the pigs belonged to the monastery, so the pigs belonged to God.

"Aunt Matilde!"

"Cecily, dear God in heaven." Her aunt, hair loosed, wimple dangling from her shoulder, came running from the mead shed. The terror in her eyes was more than Malkin could bear.

"Twasn't my fault," the swineherd whined as Malkin, still muddied and fouled, pinned him to the gate. "Master Bartholomew sent me on an errand. Gave me a coin too." As if the swineherd needed no more excuse than the promise of money to abandon his duty.

"The gate was closed when I left. I swear it." Nor were mere lads permitted to swear. But Malkin believed the sincerity in his voice. The fear that he had caused an innocent's death was not faked. No point now to raise a hue-and-cry since there appeared no malefactor against whom the villagers could give chase. She started to relax her grip.

"You can ask Thaddeus," he said, whining. "He saw Master Bartholomew. And Brother Robert, him I saw on the road."

Her aunt in the care of the village women along with Thaddeus, who still asked for "Cece" and did not understand why she did not come, Malkin heated water to bathe her niece this one last time. In front of the fire, she pulled off the soiled dress and began to wash away the mud. First from her hair, her face, her arms. As she sponged the body clean, Malkin wondered what had happened. If not the swineherd, who had opened the gate and loosed the pigs? How had Cecily come to lie face down in the ditch? Had she been trampled—though her skin bore no visible cuts—or had she fallen into the ditch and drowned in the shallow water? Had a stranger been on the road? Perchance Brother Robert had espied a newcomer?

Washing between the girl's legs, still plump with baby fat, Malkin saw a smudge of red. Blood, she thought at first. But, no, more a pigment, a spot of reddish clay that dissolved as she scrubbed it away. The color of dragonsblood, what Avicenna said resulted from the everlasting battle between dragons and elephants, one killing the other and being killed by the same, their blood mingling onto the ground.

Then, in the tender place that women did not oft speak of, but men did, especially when ale emboldened their bawdiness, Malkin saw a rawness, a bruising. Something she had never seen before when she was in charge of Cecily's baths.

An unusual mark. One that suggested to Malkin a less innocent cause of death. But who would do such a thing? How would the Abbot rule? Would the Abbot hold an inquiry since within the village—lying as it did within a mere league of the monastery—jurisdiction for all matters criminal and moral fell under his control? Or would he declare this an innocent death by drowning, since a ditch, unlike a man, could not be held to account for its misdeeds?

Fulfilling custom, Malkin sat alone with Cecily through most of the first night while her aunt lay quiet under the ministrations of Mistress Alice and her sleeping draught. The girl's body, clean and dressed in white, lay in her cradle before the low fire. For the funeral, she would be wrapped in a shroud. Mass would be said, and she'd be buried in a plain box. The priest would pray that Cecily atte Water might enter into eternal bliss and that the villagers might make wise and understand that Man does not know the hour of his death and that he should always be ready.

During the night no spirits rose, except within Malkin as she relived the day's events. The blue cloth, the body in the mud. And the mark. How long had Cecily been alone? Or had she not been alone at all? In a half-sleep, a dragon rose in her mind, wrapping itself around an elephant, its fangs cutting deep into the elephant's hide. And the elephant, falling, crushing the dragon. The weight upon her own chest, a feeling she could not breathe.

The scratch at the door brought Malkin fully awake.

"I'm here, child, to spell you." In that darkest hour before light, her aunt's neighbor and friend Alice had come. Hardly before she'd settled herself, though, Mistress Alice fell asleep in her chair, her head sinking onto her chest.

From the loft, Malkin waited, awake. She crept down and then outside, heading for the monastery in the still dark. For now the nagging had risen within her like the dragon.

Monks always rose before dawn for Matins, the first prayers of the day. All the monks would be at mass. No one else would yet be about.

Malkin slipped into the dim stairway of the abbey that led to the dormitory. No sounds except for a faraway humming. Monks praying. She walked on, the cold stone numbing her bare feet. But bare feet made less noise, and being discovered inside the halls of the monastery where outsiders, especially women, were not allowed was not an outcome she wanted to ponder. Brother Robert's room stood midway down the hall on the outer wall. She knew its location because on occasion she had seen his face from the small square window as she walked past the monastery on her way to gather plants.

She wished for a candle but dared not use one.

Entering the room she guessed was his, she stole to the window and peered out. Yes, this had to be right. Only then did she gaze about the small space, seeking something. What she did not know. The room looked even plainer than her pallet in the loft at her aunt's house. At least her coverlet was dyed the color of periwinkles, and her straw mixed with green rushes and wildflowers. Even in the dim light, she could see that the monk's blanket was coarse, a dirty brown wool, the straw dry and stale, smelling of unwashed man. No decorations lightened the walls. No books. Odd. She expected a monk would have at least one book on the stool by his bed. Instead only a candle stub sat cold in a tin cup.

Behind the door, hanging from a hook, an extra robe, nothing more.

Surely some clue could be found.

She knelt by the pallet and ran her fingers underneath the straw. She touched something. Parchment-like, but small enough to fit in the palm of her hand. She pulled it closer to her face and stood at the window to glean the beginning of day. An illustration, on vellum by the feel of it. A cherub, golden haired, the rounded face haloed by light, clothed in glorious red.

An image of Cecily, there could be no question. She tucked the vellum into her sleeve and stole out of the monastery before the bells tolled. She hid the picture in an old tree hollow. Should Brother Robert raise the alarum, should he have sensed her presence here, no evidence could be found of her theft. But would he know and accuse her?

The next day the Abbot declared the death an accident, and Malkin sat silent. What did a spot of paint now gone, a bruise, and a slip of vellum prove, especially against a man of God. She and her aunt endured the ceremony, the burial. Numbed.

On the third day Malkin roused herself. She brewed a tisane for her aunt, one to soothe grief, and laid on a new fire. With a crust of bread, she set out for the wood to gather buckthorn. For to work was a palliative.

The weaver stopped her on the road as she returned, and she shifted her load to one hip.

"A monk what died in the night. Heard he hanged himself, he did." The man's voice lowered to a whisper. "At the altar." He crossed himself as if even repeating rumors of such sacrilege would invoke the wrath of God. "His cell torn asunder as if evil spirits bedeviled him."

Evil spirits indeed. Malkin's heart squeezed so tightly she could hardly breathe. 'Twas he, then.

And for what?

She forced herself to climb the hill with her burden of buckthorn. She slipped first into the chapel and intoned her prayers, this day perhaps more fervent and with more meaning than she was wont. At the workhouse, another monk, one she did not know, took her bundle and placed a battered coin, like an absolution, onto her outstretched hand.

Valerie O. Patterson works as an attorney for the federal government. Passionate about books, she reviews children's books and is finishing an MFA in Children's Literature from Hollins University. She won a grant from the Society of Children's Book Writers and Illustrators (SCBWI) in 1998 and the Shirley Henn Award for Creative Scholarship from Hollins University in 2001 and 2005. Valerie is a member of Sisters in Crime, SCBWI, and Mystery Writers of America.

The Cozy Caprice
by Judy Pomeranz

I actually went and looked around that room at the old Cozy Caprice Motel after I heard the story. It was just as bad as you'd expect. The double bed was covered with a ratty orange spread that did nothing to hide the bumps and valleys surely created by years of unthinkable acts. A molded plastic chair sat by a particle-board bureau, and a pair of red curtains barely covered a scum-crusted window. Three wire hangers dangled from a dusty, sagging wood rod; that was the closet—not even a door. The purple shag carpet was so full of grit and sticky stuff I hated walking on it, even in my work boots. Funny thing was, there were plastic cups on the dresser with paper coverings that pronounced them "sanitary." That's about the last word you'd associate with the place.

So, what was Marla doing in a dump like that? That's a darn good question, and the answer's a story and a half.

You see, this was not something she did as a matter of course. In fact, I don't rightly suppose she'd ever done anything quite like this before. To all of us in town, she was what you might call the original good girl, sweet as could be. She was the kind of girl any of us would have been happy to have as a wife. She took care of her elderly parents and had a fine marriage and a nice house; her two beautiful teenage daughters were good students, sang in the church choir, and attended 4H; her husband, Herb, was a successful feed salesman as well as a heck of a nice fellow and good provider. He was handsome too, though going a little soft around the middle. Marla was going a little that way herself, but was still pretty as a picture. Anyway, he took good care of her, and she took good care of his house. They had a fine life. You could even say she was blessed.

So, why would she want to mess it up? What made her decide to go with my old friend Red Glover to the Cozy Caprice that afternoon? I've got some ideas, but I don't want to cast aspersions. Most folks don't believe she really wanted to be there at all. More like she was sort of compelled, like Red cast some kind of spell over her or drugged her or held his shotgun to her head. Nonsense, if you ask me.

Actually, a few of the fellows blame *The Bridges of Madison County* for her ending up in that place. Mind you, this isn't Madison County, there's not even a covered bridge for a hundred miles, but a lot of the women got ideas from that movie; that's what their men say, anyway. The husbands didn't think it was healthy, and maybe it wasn't, but I don't think that movie was responsible for what happened to Marla.

So, if we can't blame Clint Eastwood and Meryl Streep, what then? Red Glover's charm?

Hardly. Red was no Casanova. He was so shy with the women he never did marry, practically never dated. Besides, Marla'd known Red all her life. Seems odd she'd suddenly find him irresistible after all these years. Truth be told, it seems odd anyone would find Red irresistible anytime.

And we know it wasn't Herb's fault. Like I said, he was as good to Marla as could be. They were real comfortable together. He called her "mother" and she called him "daddy," whether the girls were around or not. That's how comfortable they were with one another.

So, it's got to be more complicated than that. That's why most folks blame Red.

Anyway, here's how Red told me it happened. Even though most folks don't believe him, I kind of do.

Marla was in town one afternoon. She'd been at Doc Bennett's office right there on Bell Street. She comes out Doc's door, and who does she run smack into—and I mean smack—but Red Glover.

"Hey, Marla," says Red. "How goes it?"

"Okay, Red," Marla says, looking at the sidewalk. She kept walking toward her car.

Red turned and walked alongside her. "You okay? You look kind of sad."

"I'm okay," she said, in the kind of voice that didn't give Red any reason to believe her.

"Everything go okay at Doc Bennett's?"

She stopped right there, and said, "Red, would you please leave me alone? Would you please stop prying?"

"Sorry, Marla. I didn't mean. . ."

"Please, Red."

So, Red let her walk on by herself. He just stood there and watched her march on down the street. She nodded hello to folks who greeted her, but she kept on walking, and Red, he kept on watching. Seemed very strange. He was worried; he wondered what she'd learned from Doc Bennett. Seemed, when he came to think about it, that she'd been around Doc Bennett's a lot lately.

That little worry gnawed at him, but there wasn't much he could do about it. It was none of his business, and Marla'd made that perfectly clear. Still, he'd always had a bit of an eye for Marla, as far back as when they were in grade school together, before he went into the special class. You might say he was smitten. So, he was pretty worried.

It was some days before he ran into her again. This time, it was on Main Street. And this time, he was careful to keep his counsel, if you know what I mean.

"Hey, Marla," he said, and that was that. Anything else was up to her.

"Hey, Red," she said with a smile. "Forgive me for the way I treated you the other day?"

"Sure, Marla. Everything okay now?"

"Everything's just fine now," she assured him. "Want to have a cup of coffee?"

"Okay," he said. He was surprised but real pleased she'd asked. "I'll buy you one at Mason's. Mr. Belfry just paid me." That was Red's employer at the grocery store where he worked in the stockroom.

"No, not at Mason's," she said. "I meant at my place."

Now, Red knew it was a little strange for him to go to her home in the middle of the day. Her girls would be in school, and he knew for a fact Herb was on the road—over in Jefferson County. Still, the idea of spending a little time with Marla was appealing, and they were old friends. Nothing wrong with old friends spending time together, he told himself.

"Sure, why not?" he said.

So, off they went. She drove her car; Red drove his truck.

When they arrived, she put on a pot of coffee, and they sat at the kitchen table.

"Good to see you, Red," she said, smoothing the lap of her cotton dress.

Red fidgeted with the tablecloth, twisting it between his fingers. He wondered why he felt so awkward. After all, they were just two old friends sitting in the kitchen of an afternoon, chatting, shooting the breeze.

"Real good to see you too, Marla." He had no idea what to say next.

"You okay, Red? You seem kind of nervous."

"Me? Nervous? Oh no," he lied. "Maybe just a little tired or something. Been working hard of late. Real hard. Busy season, you know."

"Right."

Then it was silent. And it wasn't one of those comfortable silences either—at least not for Red. Though from what he tells me, Marla didn't seem any too uncomfortable.

Finally the coffee stopped perking. Marla got up and poured.

"Red?" she said, as she served him.

"Yes'm?"

"Red, there's something I'd like to tell you."

"Yes?"

"I've been having some problems lately. That's why I was in to see Doc Bennett the other day."

"Problems?"

"Yes."

She didn't explain, and Red didn't feel at liberty to ask. So, he just sat there.

"And just in case anything happens," she said, "there's something I'd like you to know."

Now he had no idea what to say.

"Red, I've always liked you. Ever since we were in school. I just want you to know that."

"Same here," Red said very softly. In fact, maybe he only thought it.

"What?" she said.

"I've always liked you too," he said.

"I know that, Red. You've made that clear to me, and it means a lot. That's why I wanted to let you know how I feel."

Now, Red was no dummy, and he knew this was not something a man just lets drop, but damned if he could figure out what was supposed to come next.

"So, uh, how exactly do you feel, Marla?" As soon as his words were out, he feared she would take hers back.

"I really like you, Red. I like you an awful lot."

"Why are you telling me this?" He felt bold all of a sudden, bold enough to ask questions, and worried because of the doctor thing. "Why now? What's going on?"

"I can't tell you that. Just take what I'm saying for what it's worth. I like you in a special way, Red, and that's all there is to it."

"That's all?"

"Yes, Red. What more do you want?"

"I want to know why you're telling me this. What's wrong with you? Why were you seeing Doc Bennett?"

"Not now, Red. Let's just have our coffee now and enjoy being together. And let's keep this our little secret."

So, that was that. For the time being anyway.

Then Herb came back to town. When Red sat with him at the Rotary Club luncheon, he didn't know what to say. He felt awfully sorry for Herb, sick wife and all, but Herb seemed to be bearing it well. Didn't even mention it.

Not long after that luncheon, Herb took off again. That wasn't strange since he spent about eighty percent of his time on the road, but Red thought there was something wrong with a man who would leave a dying wife like that.

Red found himself hanging around Doc Bennett's block of Bell Street more and more. And sure enough, not two days after Herb left town, Red ran into Marla again.

"Hey, Red."

"Hey, Marla. How are you?" he asked, trying to put a meaningful stress on the words.

"I'm okay, Red,"

"Want to have a coffee at Mason's?" That was something he never would have had the nerve to ask before.

"That would be nice, Red, real nice," Marla said with a smile, the kind you could even call enticing. Her eyes stayed glued to his for what seemed quite a long time.

As they walked over to Mason's, Red began to wonder if he could have imagined the whole scene in Marla's kitchen. Had he read something into what she'd said? Maybe she meant she liked him the way she liked her girlfriends. Maybe he'd misunderstood the whole thing. Anything else was too good to think about. Except the part about her dying. That part was too awful to think about. That would have been awful at any time, but particularly so under the circumstances. More like *Love Story* than *Bridges of Madison County*.

So they sipped coffee and threw what Red interpreted as meaningful glances at each other. Marla even put her hand on his arm once. They made small talk and avoided the subject they couldn't discuss in public. Then they walked out into the square.

It was one of those glorious fall days, all cool and dry with lots of leaves falling from the trees. Red wanted, in the worst possible way, to take Marla's hand. He ached to do that, to touch just that little part of her. But he knew that was impossible here in town where everyone knew them. And, of course, he couldn't ask her to his rooming house. He was kind of hoping she'd invite him out to her place again, but she didn't. Still, he somehow sensed she wanted the same thing he did. She made that clear to him, though he still can't rightly explain how.

Then she said, very quietly, "Red, you know the old Cozy Caprice Motel?"

"Sure I do. I've always known it," he said, "but I've never been there."

The Cozy Caprice was on the highway just outside of town. No one knew the old fellow who ran the place. He lived out there and never came into town. A real loner.

"Well, Red, I thought maybe you and I could meet there some day to, you know, talk."

"Us? At the Cozy Caprice? You and me?" He wanted to be sure he understood what she was saying.

"Yes, Red. Us. It's just so hard to find a place where we can be alone to, you know, talk."

So, they agreed to go there the following afternoon. Marla asked him to pick her up, but he was smart enough to suggest they each go alone—just in case. You know, so no one would see them driving off together. Marla said not to worry about that, so he agreed to pick her up.

God knows, Red had never done anything like that before. He was awake all night feeling alternately guilty, scared, and excited. He knew there was nothing to feel guilty about, since they were only going to talk—and maybe hold hands. But to go to a place like that, well, guilt just sort of went with the territory. Now, the scared part, that made some sense. I mean, what if someone saw them? And excited? Well, of course.

Red knocked off work early the next day and swung by Marla's.

"Hey, Marla," he said as she got into his truck. She looked beautiful, all decked out in a dark blue floral print dress. It kind of took his breath away to think she had dressed like that just for him.

"Hey, Red."

And off they went to the Cozy Caprice.

It felt really strange actually pulling in there, after all the times he'd driven right by and wondered about the kind of people who would go to a place like that. He checked in at the desk and picked up a key while she waited in the truck. Then they went to the room. Red was used to his boarding house, so the room probably didn't seem as bad to him as it must have to Marla. Fact is, I don't rightly think he even noticed the room. That's not what was on his mind.

Marla sat on the orange chair, and Red sat down on that soft old bed. They just looked at one another for a few moments. Then Red reached across the short space that separated them.

"Can I hold your hand, Marla?"

She held it out to him, and he took it ever so gently. I bet he held that hand like he was holding a tiny, fragile animal. He held it and stroked it softly.

"Marla, I just want to tell you I love you. I always have."

She nodded.

"You going to be okay?" he asked quietly. "I don't think I could stand it if you weren't. Especially not now. Not after all this."

"Sure, Red. I'll be fine."

"Are you dying?"

"No, Red, I'm not dying."

"What did you mean when you said that something might 'happen' to you?"

"Later, Red. We'll talk about that later. Afterwards."

"After what?"

"Oh, Red. I know why you asked me here. Don't play games with me. It's okay, truly it is. I'm flattered you want me."

Now Red was really at a loss. He was sure she had asked him here. And she'd said it was to talk. But if she had something else in mind, he didn't want to disappoint her. That's what he told himself, anyway.

And sure enough, Marla started unbuttoning her dress. Right there. Just like that. Button after button. And all Red could do was stare.

"Am I undressing alone?" she grinned.

"No way," he said quickly, and started pulling off his own clothes.

All the while he did, though, he didn't take his eyes off Marla. She was so beautiful. All those years, he had never imagined just how beautiful she was under those clothes. Red honestly wondered—and he didn't mean it as a figure of speech—whether this was all a dream. That's what he told me. It didn't seem like anything that could actually be happening.

But it was. And I hope Red enjoyed it plenty, because his fun wasn't meant to last.

Red and Marla started going at it, so to speak—Red mostly stunned, Marla seemingly very excited. Red was flattered and proud when she screamed her pleasure at the top of her lungs, loud as you please.

And then it happened, the kind of thing that always has to happen in this kind of a situation with a guy like Red. The door flew open, and Police Chief Flagg burst in.

Now, Red hoped he was dreaming.

Marla screamed more and more. Didn't she know what was happening, Red wondered. How could her ecstasy go on like that, with the chief right there.

Then he realized it wasn't what you'd call ecstasy. Her cries were cries of hurt, of pain. Tears flowed from her eyes. She screamed at Red to get off her, to leave her alone. She screamed at Chief Flagg to help her, to get Red away from her. Please, please, please help me. Help me.

Chief Flagg pulled his pistol on Red, maybe the first time in a decade he's had occasion to draw that gun. He told Red, in the strongest possible way, to get off her and get dressed. All the while, he kept the gun pointed at Red.

Then he told Marla to get her clothes on, but he told her in the gentlest possible tone. Red was partly confused, but mostly just plain scared. It was one of those experiences that makes your life flash in front of your eyes, and Red's did. There wasn't all that much worth viewing in that simple life, but Red had the presence of mind to know that what flashed by was one hundred percent preferable to what was to come.

Chief Flagg radioed his deputy to get on down there right away, and he was there in minutes. Deputy Striker took the sobbing Marla home, and Chief Flagg took a speechless Red down to the station.

And that's the story, just the way Red told it to me. Seems no one else would listen to him. Of course not. Marla's Marla, and Red's Red, and that's the way these things work.

So, what happened here? What brought the police? Well, it turns out the old man in the motel had called the police to tell them he thought he heard a rape going on. If you ask me, it's funny he'd do that, since there was no rape going on and since that kind of activity, we all know, goes on in that kind of place all the time.

But call he did. So I think someone must have put him up to it. Probably paid him. Only stands to reason. But the police never thought of that. Chief Flagg just thought the old man was being a good citizen, responding to cries of distress.

So, Red went to jail. Poor fellow was pretty sure he deserved to be there, since he knew what he had done with Marla was wrong. It was adultery, and that was a sin. Still, there was a part of him that felt like a stay in jail might not be too high a price to pay for the experience.

But it was still very puzzling to him, the way Marla had reacted.

Well, next thing you know, Marla's pregnant. Wouldn't you just know it? And it was confirmed by Doc Bennett himself. No doubt about it. And we know the seed wasn't Herb's because we all know he's not been able to make babies for years. Medically impossible.

Poor Marla, everyone said. Poor Marla. Raped and with child, the child of a rapist. A tiny, horrible reminder of that terrible experience.

Maybe she'd have an abortion, some people figured. But no, Marla had a strong religious feeling against that. Good thing too, since Doc Bennett doesn't do abortions. She'd have had to go several counties away—probably to the capital—to get that kind of thing done. Mostly, the town at large doesn't believe in it, and Marla's a good, moral person that way.

Well, that little baby on the way was just too much. Marla's marriage couldn't take that kind of strain. She couldn't talk to Herb about all this, and he was just as glad since he's not good in that kind of situation. And she was unable to give herself to her husband, if you know what I mean, after this defilement and the lasting evidence of it in the form of that child inside her. Old Herb didn't know how to react, didn't know what to do, how to make anything right again. Turned out he couldn't. Marla's girls were mostly just embarrassed, and that about says it all for them. So that nice, blessed little family was finally broken up over all this.

But there's a happy ending here—for Marla anyway.

It seemed Doc Bennett, who was caring for Marla, started to kind of take to her, and she to him. After a little time passed, they decided to tie the knot themselves.

Our town's as pleased as can be for Marla, glad she's been able to pull herself together and salvage a bit of happiness from this tragedy. Even Herb is happy for her, or as happy as he's capable of being at this point.

And that little baby sure enough did come along—and a couple months early. Yes, he was early, but as big and healthy as you please. So, maybe someone's still smiling down on our Marla, still casting blessings down on her.

And you know the strangest thing, the nicest blessing of all? That little baby even looks like his new daddy. He looks just like Doc Bennett.

It's a miracle, they say.

Judy Pomeranz is a freelance writer, lecturer, and art critic. Her articles have appeared in a wide range of newspapers and magazines and her short stories and essays have been published in literary journals including Santa Barbara Review, Potomac Review, Crescent Review, Fodderwing, *and* MasAve Review, *as well as in the anthologies,* Great Writers, Great Stories, *and* Chesapeake Crimes. *Her novella,* On the Far Edge of Love: New York Stories, *is being serialized in élan magazine, which recently serialized her earlier novellas,* Lies Beneath the Surface *and* Elegy. *She holds a MA in writing from Johns Hopkins University, teaches writing at Georgetown University, and has won prizes and recognition in fiction contests sponsored by The National Press Club, the D.C. Bar, and élan magazine.*

Mother Love
by Harriette I. Sackler

It all began, not on the proverbial dark and stormy night, but rather on an overcast and frigid morning in February. Not being a winter person in the best of times, it took superhuman effort for me to weather the elements and go to work. Another season like this and I'd be forced to consider relocating to a warmer clime.

No sooner did I stomp into the front office of Rolling Hills Middle School then Sylvia, our administrative assistant, informed me that John Greene, the school's principal, had been looking for me.

As I entered his office, I noticed that John looked particularly somber. Since he was usually a jovial and outgoing guy, I figured something was wrong, hopefully not of my doing.

"Hey, Sherry, thanks for coming in." John waved me to a chair. "I wanted to talk to you about Jimmy Moore. . .."

"Don't tell me he's in trouble again! What'd he do this time? Rob a bank?"

"No," John chuckled. "I almost wish that were the case. I got a call this morning from a Nina Clement. She's Jimmy's aunt. Last night at about eleven, Jimmy's mother was assaulted on her way downtown. She's employed by an office cleaning service and works after hours. The injuries were fatal and she died in the ambulance. Real nasty business. Jimmy has two younger sibs, you know. Three kids with no mother now. Jesus, what a world. Anyway, I wanted you to know first thing. I'd appreciate your representing the school at the funeral on Friday."

"Oh, John, I'm so sorry." I felt guilty for assuming the worst about Jimmy. "Of course, I'll do whatever I can."

"Thanks, Sherry. Keep me posted. The aunt said the kids are staying with her. Jimmy'll be back in school on Monday."

Damnit! It seemed that a day didn't go by without news of one tragedy or another. The randomness of street crime was frightening, especially in this part of town. As if being poor wasn't enough.

I counsel middle-schoolers in an urban working-class neighborhood. I don't have any spoiled, over-privileged prima donnas on my caseload. My students lead a more back-to-basics existence. They play stickball in the street, have paper routes to earn spending money, and don't sport clothes or shoes with designer labels and fat price tags.

After a morning filled with meetings and phone calls, I found some time to pull out Jimmy Moore's file. My contact with him had been extensive. Though a bright young man, he had a history of authority conflicts and oppositional behavior. Jimmy took issue with directives given him by staff and his classroom teachers considered him a disruptive influence.

For my part, I found Jimmy to be engaging. Though closed and uncommunicative about himself, he possessed a sharp sense of humor and made astute observations about the world. I liked him.

From conversations with White Elementary's school counselor, I had learned that Jimmy's nine-year old brother, Michael, functioned on level in the fourth grade. He presented him as a quiet boy, somewhat remote, but very polite and cooperative. Annie was six, in first grade, and an adorable little girl.

Mom was a plain, dowdy, heavyset woman, and extremely vocal about her rough life. She held a job to help support the family, took care of the home and children, and had deep feelings about being short-changed in life.

The kids were a handful and didn't cooperate or behave as she wanted them to. I had never met Mr. Moore, nor had White's counselor. However, according to his wife, he was a marginal provider and not involved in childrearing.

As it turned out, Mrs. Moore's funeral was not held until the following Tuesday. A back-up in the Medical Examiner's office delayed the autopsy. I learned that severe blows to the head caused Mrs. Moore's fatal injuries. While the weapon still had not been identified, several imbedded splinters suggested she had been bludgeoned with a heavy wooden object. To date no leads had been reported.

The service was held at Mt. Ivy Cemetery. The cold, sunny afternoon held no foreboding of the snow predicted to hit the region within a day or two. A small number of mourners gathered around the gravesite. Only one modest floral arrangement rested on the plain, unadorned casket.

Jimmy stood with his family on the opposite side of the grave. He wore a flimsy jacket, and I had the urge to take off my quilted coat and cover him. The two younger children stood on either side of him. Jimmy's arms were protectively thrown over their shoulders.

About two feet away stood a man whom I assumed was the children's father. He was tall, maybe just shy of six feet, and painfully bent, as though, like Atlas, he carried a heavy burden on his shoulders. His nose, red-tinged from an abundance of broken capillaries, indicated he was no stranger to the bottle. His eyes were bloodshot and I noticed a slight tremor in the hands he loosely clasped in front of him. He looked like a failed man. A husband and father who never quite made the grade.

The minister began to speak and I forced myself to focus on his words. Within moments, it became obvious that he knew very little, if anything, about the deceased. No one else came forward to offer words and the service ended shortly after it began.

I decided to take advantage of the invitation to go back to the Moore home for post-funeral refreshments. It would give me the opportunity to speak to Mr. Moore and the children.

The house resembled the hundreds of others in the neighborhood, but the exterior looked shabbier than most. As I entered the front door, a bubbly woman I recognized from the funeral greeted me.

"Well, hello. Thank you so much for coming, Miss. . . ."

"Oh, I'm Sherry Levin, counselor at Jimmy's middle school. And, on behalf of our staff, I'd like to offer sincere condolences to the Moores."

"Well, thank you, honey. By the way, I'm Nina Clement, Jimmy's aunt. My late husband Henry and Jimmy's mom were brother and sister. Henry passed eight years ago—just up and died from a stroke. I guess all those cigarettes and beers finally did him in. Anyway, sure is sad about Ellen. But maybe she'll be at peace now 'cause she sure wasn't when she was alive."

"I'm so sorry to hear that," I stuttered. My head spun from so much information. "How are the children doing?"

"Oh, they're doin' just fine. They've been stayin' with me and gettin' lots of lovin'. They're angels, you know. Treat 'em just as though they were my own. Henry and me couldn't have little ones, so these three have always been close to my heart. By the way, I guess you'd like to say a word to John, so let me round him up and bring him over."

A moment later Mr. Moore came ambling over. He thanked me for coming, but seemed uncomfortable and at a loss for words. He didn't mention his wife, but rather praised Nina Clement for taking over the responsibilities of making funeral arrangements and watching over the children.

"Jimmy, I want to tell you that the staff and students at the school have been thinking about you and your family. I asked you to visit with me so that if there's anything you'd like to talk about, I'm here for you. The past few weeks had to be very rough and maybe you could use a helping hand in sorting out your feelings."

My heart went out to the young man sitting in the chair next to mine. Jimmy had just returned to school the day before, but I had given him a day to get settled before meeting with him. He looked so vulnerable, so confused.

"I guess I don't know what to talk about," he whispered, looking down at the floor.

"Well, I noticed at the funeral that you have a handsome brother and a lovely sister. Would you like to tell me about them?"

For the first time since entering my office, Jimmy looked up at me.

"Yeah, they're great. I love 'em a lot." His affection for his siblings was well reflected in just a few words and the proud tone of his voice.

"The three of you must be very sad losing your mom."

In astonishment, I witnessed an incredible change take place in Jimmy's affect. His whole body tensed. His fists clenched. His expression hardened. I felt a flutter of anxiety in my chest and drew in a deep breath to dispel the uncomfortable sensation.

"I hated her. She hurt us and I'm glad she's dead."

Startled, it took me a minute to respond, afraid of what I was about to hear. "How did she hurt you?"

"She hit us. Yelled at us. Punished us even when we didn't do anything wrong. Annie and Bobby were so scared of her all the time. They're so little. What could they do that was so bad?"

I felt sick, but I continued on. "Jimmy, did anyone else know about what your mom did? Your dad? A neighbor?"

"My dad works a lot. He's not home most of the time and when he is, he's sleeping. Once in a while we get to have supper with him and maybe even watch TV together. But he's always so tired. And things happened when he wasn't around."

"Is there anyone else who might have known?"

"Yeah, Aunt Nina did. It made her angry and she tried to get Mom to stop. But it didn't work. So she always tried to have us spend a lot of time at her house."

I needed time to think. "I'm so very sorry, for you, Annie, and Bobby. Let's talk more about this tomorrow."

As he rose from his chair, Jimmy turned to me and smiled. "Thanks, Miss Levin. You're a good guy." With that, he left my office.

I slept poorly that night, spending a lot of time thinking about Jimmy. At six in the morning, I managed to drag myself into the shower, dress, and down three cups of strong coffee.

Within the hour I arrived at my office. Staff had not yet begun filtering in. The janitor was the only person on board at such an early hour and he greeted me warmly.

"Morning, Miz Levin," he saluted me as though we were in the military.

"Good morning, Mr. Ryan. You're up and about early today."

"Can certainly say the same about you. Busy day ahead?"

"You know it. I figured I might as well get a head start before the troops arrived."

"Well, you have a nice day, you hear?" Mr. Ryan started down the hall, broom in hand.

Just as I turned to enter my office, he called after me.

"Hey, Miz Levin, you hear the news this morning?"

"No, I'm afraid not. In fact, I never even thought to turn on the radio. Something interesting happen?"

"You might say that, I suppose," he answered. "Reports say the police caught the guy who killed that lady. You know, the one who has a kid here. Seems some fellow tried to mug a woman 'bout one this morning. But she was a fighter, bless her heart, and started to scream at the top of her lungs. Some folks at an all-night coffee shop down the block heard her and came running. The guy behind the counter called the police. This thug has a record as long as your arm—assault, theft, all sorts of things. Woman says he tried to bop her with a wood board."

"Thank you, thanks a lot, Mr. Ryan, for sharing the news with me. You've made my day."

I had come into school on a picture perfect August day to prepare for the new term. As I strolled past the yard, I noticed a group of boys involved in a boisterous game of basketball. Jimmy Moore was among them. After scoring the winning point, he saw me, waved, and trotted over.

"Hi, Miss Levin! Hope you're having a great summer." He smiled at me with a warmth that lit up his face. Over the months, Jimmy had blossomed.

"Hey! You look like you've been doing great! Everything okay at home?"

"You bet. We've got a good thing going now. Say, why don't you stop by the house? Aunt Nina's home today."

"You know, Jimmy, I think I will. It's a gorgeous day and I'm up for a walk. Thanks for the invite."

From my sessions with Jimmy prior to the close of the school year, I learned that Aunt Nina had moved in with the Moores to care for the children and, though hard to believe, planned to tie the knot with Jimmy's father. Mr. Moore, it seemed, was transforming into a real family man and showing some sides of himself that hadn't been evident before. All seemed well with the world.

As I rang the doorbell of the much-improved Moore home, I heard an exclamation of delight from within.

"Well, I'll be! If it isn't Miz Levin come to call. Come in, come in. Let's sit over an iced tea and talk."

"Hi, Mrs. Clement. I ran into Jimmy at the school and he suggested I stop by. Wow, what a difference. I'm thrilled for all of you."

"Ain't it the truth! I couldn't ask for anything more. Three great kids, a good man, a nice home. What could be better?"

"Are you home full-time or working too, Mrs. Clement?" I asked.

"Oh, I like to be home with the kids, but I'll be startin' a part-time job when school's on. I'll be workin' at the Sports Shack over on Main and Third. Looking forward to it, truth be told. I'm not a bad athlete, you know."

"No, I didn't know that. What do you play?"

"Well, in my younger days I traveled with a woman's baseball league. Didn't make much money, but it sure was a hoot. Had quite a followin' back then. "'Super Slammin Nina' they called me. The best hitter in the league." With a look of pride, amusement, and something I couldn't put my finger on she said, "Had a swing that could kill."

Harriette Sackler is a lifelong fan of the mystery and teaches several adult courses on the genre. She is a member of Sisters in Crime Chesapeake Chapter and serves as Grants Chair on the Malice Domestic Board of Directors.

As Assistant Director of Community Resources and Development at a residential treatment center for children and adolescents with severe emotional disabilities, she spends a great deal of time writing public relations materials and newsletters.

Harriette and her husband live in Montgomery County, Maryland, with their three pampered Bichon fluffs. They have two lovely grown daughters.

Driven to Distraction
by Marcia Talley

When Harrison keeled over and died I didn't think I'd marry again, but Mama said, "Life goes on, Marjorie Ann. When you fall off a horse, you have to climb right back on."

Given a chance, Mama would have matched me up with one of Harrison's law partners, right there at South River Country Club as they converged on the roast beef carving station after the funeral. But I have my pride. I waited a respectable year before marrying Stephen, who swept me off my feet with the lean, rawboned, good looks of a Montana rancher, a laid-back wrangler who spoke fluent U.S. Tax Code. The way Stephen handled Harrison's estate was nothing short of dazzling.

Stephen was clever with gadgets too. In his office at home, he had a desktop computer, a laptop, a scanner, three monitors—one as big as an over-the-sofa painting of the Last Supper—two cameras that scanned the room like disembodied eyeballs, and wires that snaked kudzu-like around the table legs. I pretty much kept out until cleaning day when I'd have to run the vacuum and dust his office myself. Theresa refused. The blinking and beeping unnerved her. She was convinced the machines would steal her thoughts, and to tell the truth, I half agreed with her.

The last thing Stephen needed was another piece of electronics, so for his fortieth birthday I gave him a fabulous five-course dinner at Northwoods Restaurant and a gift card from American Express. He reached across his créme caramel, gathered up my hand and pressed it to his lips, his green eyes flashing "thank you" in the candlelight. By the way he glanced at his watch, I suspected he wanted to skip the after-dinner glass of Remy Martin and rush straight off to the mall to cash it in, but, fortunately, the mall had already closed.

I hoped he'd use the card at Nordstrom or Eddie Bauer, but the next morning Stephen left the house early and was probably waiting at Circuit City when the doors slid open. He came home lugging a box labeled MapMasterIV and spent the rest of Saturday morning holed up in his office, reading the manual. After lunch, he plopped his new toy onto the dashboard of his pickup and drove off, happy as a clam.

Sunday morning when I eased into the passenger seat of the BMW, I found Stephen balancing the MapMasterIV on his knees. He plugged its cord into the cigarette lighter socket and jiggled what I took to be an aerial up and down. He leaned sideways, so close I could smell his Drakkar Noir aftershave, adjusted the MapMaster on its bean bag base, positioned the whole shebang on the dashboard, and punched a few buttons. Then he backed carefully out of the driveway, grinning.

"Just listen," he said.

Drive point two miles west and turn right.

The MapMaster was female and she spoke in a calm, nonjudgmental voice, like the 411 information lady.

Obediently, Stephen turned right onto Dogwood Lane. "It'll direct us to church."

"You know how to get to church."

"Of course I know how to get to church, Marjorie Ann, but it's interesting to see how the MapMaster will route us."

Drive one point seven miles south and turn right.

Stephen tilted the MapMaster slightly in my direction so I could see the bright yellow display. He tapped the screen with his index finger. "Here's our route in pink. That's the interstate over there, in red," he explained, as if I were a particularly slow and difficult child.

Continue point five miles and take ramp right.

Stephen flipped on his turn signal and eased the car onto the interstate. "It's fantastic technology." He beamed. "Uses the global positioning system. It gloms onto satellites, figures out where you are, then gives you driving directions." He waved a hand. "It comes preprogrammed with hotels and restaurants, or you can put in a street address. . ." His voice trailed off. "I've got it programmed for St. Margarets."

Drive four point one miles and exit right.

I watched as Allen Parkway, our usual turnoff, receded in my side view mirror. "Why didn't you turn back there, Stephen?"

Stephen stared straight ahead, one hand resting lightly on top of the steering wheel. "I wanted to see where Marilyn would route us."

"Marilyn?"

"MapMaster. M. M. Get it?"

I rolled my eyes toward heaven. Where in the marriage vows did I promise to cherish a guy who names his toys after dead movie stars? I sighed. "Well, I can understand why, uh, Marilyn might be helpful if you're driving in a strange city and don't know where you're going," I grumbled. "But if you already know the way, why waste time fooling around?" I swiveled the screen toward me and studied the buttons: Find, Route, Menu.

"Don't mess with it, Marjorie Ann! You'll screw up the settings."

"Okay, okay." I raised both hands in self-defense. "I won't touch your precious whatzit." I folded my arms across my chest and settled into my seat, wishing I could turn on the radio, but I knew better. Stephen wouldn't be able to hear MM over the sound of NPR.

A few minutes later, MM chirped, In *four hundred feet turn right.*

Stephen pulled off the expressway and, following MM's instructions, wound through a public housing project and an industrial neighborhood until at last, by some miracle, we turned onto a street I recognized and I could see St. Margaret's steeple directly ahead.

Arriving at destination on right.

"Well I'll be darned," I said.

Stephen eased into the parking lot, switched off the ignition and grinned like a schoolboy. "Ain't technology grand?"

Even Reverend Nelson's interminable sermon on life lessons to be learned from the parable of the Prodigal Son didn't dampen Stephen's enthusiasm for his new toy. After the benediction, he hustled me out to the car, not even pausing on the chapel steps to shake the good Reverend's meaty hand.

"We need to stop at the store for toilet paper," I reminded my husband somewhat breathlessly. "And milk."

Stephen drove the few blocks to our Whole Foods market and waited while I went into the store. When I returned to the parking lot carrying my purchases, Stephen demonstrated how to set a waypoint.

"You just drive where you want to go, Marjorie Ann, and press the Mark button." A number popped up on the screen. "Now you use this rocker pad to rename the waypoint. W...H...O... There. Whole Foods." Looking over his shoulder, I noticed that Stephen had already set up waypoints for his office, Home Depot, Golds Gym, B&B Yachts, and our home, of course. He punched the waypoint labeled "Home" and peeled out of the parking lot, tires squealing.

Between Whole Foods and Home, the bypass around the construction site on Truman Street threw MM for a loop.

Off route. Recalculating.

"Why did it do that?" I asked.

"It's a new road, Marjorie Ann. Marilyn doesn't know about it."

MM dutifully recalculated and wanted us to go up Route 2 and take the Route 100 bypass, but Stephen decided not to.

Off route. Recalculating.

The woman was far more patient with my husband than I was.

As soon as possible, make a U-turn, she recommended politely.

"You could make money," I mused, "designing special voices for this thing."

"What do you mean?"

"You can already select a language," I said. "So why not come up with some alternate voice chips like the nagging wife. Instead of saying 'off route, recalculating,' she'd say, 'You missed the turn, you idiot! But do you ever listen to me? Nooooh.'"

The corner of Stephen's mouth twitched upward.

"Or," I continued, warming to my invention, "you could punch in a waypoint for your mother. Then every time you bypassed her house it's 'So, Mr. Bigshot. How come you never visit your mother? Make a U-turn. Now!'"

Stephen joined in, dredging up a Beavis and Butthead voice from somewhere in his reckless youth. "Whoa, dude, like there's a fork in the road. Huh huh huh. Fork. Get it?" He chuckled, a rare event, and turned to study me over the rims of his sunglasses. "You patent that, Marjorie Ann, and we can both retire to the south of France."

Truth is, Stephen made excellent money as the head of his own firm. We could retire to the south of France like, any minute, if he wanted, but Stephen preferred to spend his money and his spare time on boating or golfing or off-roading in the Arizona desert. The previous weekend he'd dragged me to the GM dealership to check out a Humvee. As if.

I squirmed in my seat. MM had selected a route home that didn't involve a freeway. If she didn't hurry up, the milk would spoil. "I think you should just go straight up 32," I said, feeling testy.

Stephen ignored me.

"I'll bet this route is ten minutes longer."

"Than?"

"Than going straight up 32."

"Where's your sense of adventure, Marjorie Ann?"

"I don't know, Stephen. I think I lost it back in 1998."

MM was feeling testy, too. *Off route. Recalculating* .

Stephen slapped his palm against the steering wheel. "Damn!"

I flinched. "Why'd she say that?"

"I missed the exit. I was listening to you, Marjorie Anne. Can't you keep quiet even for a minute?"

I turned my head and glared out the passenger-side window, my eyes shooting darts into the trees, my mouth clamped shut, feeling glad that Stephen was leaving town the next day for the annual AICPA tech conference in Las Vegas. He was giving a talk on the paperless office. Paperless, ha! Good thing nobody at the AICPA had to empty Stephen's wastepaper basket or they'd ask for their money back.

I would have gone along—the Venetian Hotel has lagoons with gondolas floating through it, et mind-blowing cetera—but mama was having an eyelift and I felt obliged to stay home and hold her hand. So, while Stephen spent his days holed up in frigid conference rooms and his nights playing blackjack on the Strip, I spent mine fetching and toting for mama. I bundled up her newspapers for recycling, cleaned out her refrigerator, and scoured the shelves at Blockbuster for Russell Crowe DVDs. She invited me to the film fest, but I think it was because she wanted me to make the popcorn.

Midweek, I was taking a break from mama and getting a pedicure when she rang through on my cell phone.

"Can you pick up Elroy in Shady Side?"

Elroy was mama's handyman. His truck had "broke

down" and mama was too hopped up on pain killers to drive down there herself.

I didn't feel like going anywhere and told her so.

"Do you want to pick dead leaves out of my swimming pool, Marjorie Ann? Or mow the lawn?" Without waiting for an answer, mama started rattling off directions to Elroy's, but I tuned out about halfway through. I had Elroy's address. I had Stephen's MapMaster. Piece of cake.

Stephen had left the MapMaster locked up in his truck, so when I got home from the beauty parlor, I moved it into the BMW. When I plugged it in, MM politely informed me she was acquiring her satellites, then waited for me to press Find, then Addresses. I used the rocker key to spell out, number by number and letter by letter, Elroy's address, then pressed Go To.

MM, bless her little batteries and computer chip heart, got me to Elroy's and back to mama's without a hitch.

I was backing down her driveway, mere seconds from a clean getaway, when mama popped out her front door, waving her arms. "Trash bags, Marjorie Ann! I need heavy-duty trash bags. And bug spray!" I waggled my fingers so she'd know I'd heard her, then punched Home Depot into the MapMasterIV.

I hardly ever go to Home Depot, especially from mama's house, so it didn't particularly surprise me when MM directed me off the freeway and onto a quiet street in Morningside Heights. I was surprised when she advised me to turn right into a cul-de-sac and absolutely astonished when MM announced that I was arriving at destination, smack dab in front of a cute little Dutch colonial.

I recognized the house. It belonged to Cheryl, from church. She sang in the choir with Stephen. At the Ferguson wedding they'd sung a duet, "One Hand, One Heart," and there hadn't been a dry eye in the house.

Why had Stephen set a waypoint for Cheryl? I felt dizzy, wondering if all the hours they'd spent practicing

"One Hand, One Heart" had escalated into Two Hands, Big Breasts.

Deeply suspicious, I selected the waypoint Stephen had set up for Gold's Gym and pushed Go To. MM directed me out of the cul-de-sac, back onto the freeway and through the center of town. Gold's Gym had long disappeared from my rear view mirror when MM instructed me to turn into Foxcroft Acres, a new development on the south side of town.

Arriving at destination on right.

I eased my foot onto the brake and stared at the name on the mailbox: J. Barton. I recognized that name, too. The "J" stood for Julie and she was Stephen's personal trainer.

So, Julie had set up private practice in her home? Helping my husband with his pushups perhaps? If Stephen hadn't been in Las Vegas, I would have beaned him with one of his own five-pound, handheld dumbbells.

I slammed the accelerator to the floor and peeled out of there. Mama's trash bags and bug spray would just have to wait.

The waypoints labeled "T&E" and "Russell" turned out to be just that, the Art Deco building housing the city's most prominent accounting firm and the office of Russell Herman, Stephen's attorney, respectively. But when I followed MM's directions for B&B Yachts, she took me miles out of town, down Route 214 and onto a narrow country road that ended in a long wooden pier.

Arriving at destination.

The BMW's tires crunched on the gravel as I eased onto the shoulder and cut the engine. Just ahead, at the water's edge, stood a cluster of summer cottages that had been converted into year-around homes. A child of perhaps three or four rode a tricycle around and around on the blacktopped driveway of a white clapboard rancher adjacent to the pier. I scrunched down in the driver's seat and watched the kid pop wheelies, my head swimming. What the hell was going on?

Almost immediately, the garage door yawned open and

a woman appeared, her hair a nimbus of gold against the dark interior behind her. I scrunched down even further. When I dared to peek again, she had hustled the kid into a car seat and was backing her PT Cruiser out of the garage and down the drive.

B&B Yachts? Hah! I knew what was going on. Stephen was leading a double life. He probably had mistresses, maybe even wives and children, scattered all across the city. The county. The state of Maryland. Maybe even the world!

After all I'd done for the SOB! I watched the dust kicked up by his girlfriend's tires swirl down the road behind me and remembered a moment just before our wedding, at the rehearsal dinner. I had been leaning over the sink in the ladies room, touching up my lip liner, when mama took me aside and in one of those priceless mother-daughter moments, came the closest she ever came to discussing sex with me. "Remember, Marjorie Ann, give a man steak at home and he won't go out for hamburger." Well, I'd been giving Stephen filet mignon twice a week since our honeymoon, so what the hell was he going out for? Tenderloin?

When the dust had settled, I climbed out of the car, hoping that a walk in the spring sunshine might clear the sick visions out of my head. I strolled to the end of the road and stepped onto the pier. To my left, three sailboats bobbed quietly, water chuckling softly along their sleek fiberglass hulls. To my right, a half dozen kayaks were lined up on a narrow strip of sand, each stern bearing a TWHA stencil to show that they belonged to the Truxton Woods Homeowners' Association. If I took one out for a paddle, probably nobody would notice or care.

I reached the end of the pier and sat down on the rough boards, dangling my feet over the water. A soft breeze lifted my hair and cooled the hot tears that streamed down my cheeks. I turned my face toward the afternoon sun. As far as I was concerned, Stephen could take a long walk off a short pier.

I sat up straight. Where had that come from? Perhaps the snowy egret elegantly fishing in the shallows had whispered the suggestion into my ear. A long walk off a short pier. I scrambled to my feet, brushed off the seat of my slacks and hurried back to the car to fetch MM.

With the MapMaster tucked under one arm, I returned to the beach and selected what appeared to be the most seaworthy kayak. I switched MM to battery power, then laid it carefully on the bottom of the boat. I plopped down on the sand, rolled up my pant legs, removed my shoes, and set them next to MM. When I was confident nobody was looking, I eased the kayak into the water, climbed aboard, and paddled to a spot about fifty feet off the end of the pier where I figured the water would be nice and deep. I balanced the paddle across the gunwales and lifted MM onto my lap, my thumbs hovering over her array of buttons.

I had been half listening when Stephen showed me how to set a waypoint; I hoped I wouldn't foul it up. Following his instructions as I remembered them, I punched the Mark button to capture my present location, somewhere in the middle of Calvert Creek. When MM asked me to, I used the rocker pad to scroll through the letters, carefully relabeling my new waypoint, "B&B Yachts," and obliterating the old one.

When Stephen came home from Vegas on Friday it was all I could do to remain civil, wondering with whom he'd shared his king-sized bed at the Venetian, wondering who had been his lucky charm at the blackjack tables, wondering who had been his partner for the two-for-the-price-of-one buffet dinner special at the Mirage. I could hardly bear for Stephen to touch me, wondering as his fingers caressed my cheek exactly where those hands had been lately.

Monday night, no surprise, Stephen called on his cell phone to say he wouldn't be home for dinner.

"Where are you now?" I asked.

"Just leaving the gym and heading back to the office."

In the background, MM chimed in. *In point three miles take ramp right.*

I paused, doing my own recalculation. Ramp right. From his gym to the office was a straight shot down Fairmont. No right ramps anywhere in that scenario. "I see," I said, each word a frozen shard.

"It's tax season, Marjorie Ann. Need I remind you? I'm working late. I have a lot to do."

Drive one point three miles then exit left.

Where had I seen an exit left recently? Ah, yes. On the way to whomever lived at "B&B Yachts."

Inside me, something snapped. "Lies, Stephen. All lies."

"What are you talking about, Marjorie Ann?"

I held the receiver to my ear, silently seething, listening to Stephen pile excuse upon sorry excuse while in the background, turn by turn, MM was confirming what I already knew. In a few minutes, Stephen would be heading down a dark, dusty country road, where a beautiful blonde awaited him in a white clapboard rancher adjacent to a pier.

"Marjorie Ann? You still there?"

"As far as I'm concerned, Stephen, you can go straight to hell!"

"You can't..." Stephen began, followed by, "What the—?" and seconds later by the nearly simultaneous explosions of shattered glass and deploying airbags.

And MM's voice, softly reassuring. *Arriving at destination.*

Marcia Talley is the Agatha and Anthony Award-winning author of six Hannah Ives mysteries including This Enemy Town *and* Through the Darkness, *all set in the Chesapeake Bay region. She is author/editor of two star-studded collaborative*

serial novels, Naked Came the Phoenix *and* I'd Kill For That, *set in a fashionable health spa and an exclusive gated community, respectively. Her prize-winning short stories appear in more than a dozen collections, including* Blood on Their Hands *(Berkley, 2003),* Death by Dickens *(Berkley, 2004),* Thou Shalt Not Kill *(Carroll and Graf, 2005),* Baltimore Noir *(Akashic, 2006), and* The World's Finest Mystery and Crime Stories *(Forge, 2003, 2004). She lives in Annapolis, Maryland, one of the finest places in the world to indulge her passion for sailing.*

The Blonde in Black
by Sandi Wilson

"So how'd you get out of the basement?" asked Nate, who'd just come in from his AA group at Georgetown Episcopal up the street. He'd only heard the last few bits, enough to know that our mutual friend Jynx Devereaux had spent last night in the haunted, two hundred-year-old home of a mega-wealthy author of unauthorized celebrity biographies who—surprise!—had made all kinds of enemies over the years.

"There was a servant's staircase in the back by the coal cellar," Jynx answered. "Creaky and creepy. Musta walked through a bajillion cobwebs. Nobody had used those steps in years."

"Wonder why the poltergeists didn't lock that door too?" asked Stella.

Jynx shook her head. "I don't know. It's odd."

"What kind of sounds did you hear from the attic?" I asked.

"Like some monster dragging a big ball and chain," she said. For someone who'd just lived through a night of terror with otherworldly beings in a storied mansion in the heart of Georgetown, Jynx seemed pretty calm.

"What is it? What's different about this place?" Nate scraped a chair over and put his long feet up on it. Jynx spent many nights in places that were haunted, and we'd all heard the hair-raising tales.

Jynx paused, then answered, "It's just too...I don't know, like a bad horror movie. Faucets start running. Books fly off the shelves. Papers blow around. And noises up in the attic! I mean come on, can't they think of something original?"

144

"Well, I don't know about you guys, but this whole thing gives me the heebie-jeebies," said Stella. Stella and Mickey were also in AA. Recovering alcoholics have kept the coffee industry perking.

"Yeah, well, I sure wouldn't go in that house, no matter how rich she is," said Mickey. "Was it just the two of you in there, with all those spirits?"

"Uh-huh. Her son went across the street to his friend's house for a sleepover. She said he's totally freaked out by this."

Jynx looked at me as the others clamored on about spirits, well-known psychic and spiritualist, she was as pretty as a supermodel, with skin the color of creamy café mocha, black hair cut short and sticking out in little peaks and tweaks all over her head.

"And you all know that Georgetown has more essesseff than any other part of D.C.," Mickey asserted.

"Essess—who?" asked Nate.

"S.S.F., you idiot. Spirits per square foot."

"You just say that because you live here. What about Old Town Alexandria?"

"Well, let's ask Maggie," Mickey said, "who just moved into the San Leandro, where, as we all know, the Blonde in Black resides."

All heads turned toward me. It was no secret that my Aunt Delilah had left me her Georgetown apartment after she died, and that I'd sold my house in Glover Park and moved in a few months ago.

"It's 1946. A beautiful young bride leaps to her death from the top of San Leandro's old tower," Mickey said in a deep radio announcer's voice. "Or was she murdered? Some folks say they heard the young woman screaming up on the roof, and that her husband pushed her over the edge. And here's the other weird part: Nobody ever saw him after that day. What happened to him?"

"Maggie, is that true?" asked Nate.

I shrugged my shoulders.

Mickey said, "She might've lived in your apartment, you know."

"And you might be jumping to the Isle of Conclusions, you know?" I snapped back. "Look, real estate people will stop at nothing to get top dollar for these places. It's a woo-woo ghosty legend, which, if it's far enough back, is good for sales. Especially in this market, with all these overpriced condos."

"What's 'far enough back'?" asked Nate.

"Fifty-eight years," Mickey snapped. "That's the point when a ghost isn't scary anymore. I read it in *Forbes.*"

Everyone laughed, and I was grateful for the diversion.

"Did your aunt ever mention it to you? About the Blonde in Black, I mean?" Stella asked me.

I felt my lower lip quiver and raised my coffee cup to hide it. I shook my head, but not soon enough for Mickey.

"She did tell you!" he said.

"She did not," I said.

Truth was, she didn't have to. I always knew.

Aunt Delilah used to invite me to stay with her for a few weeks every summer, usually around the Fourth of July. My parents would drive here from the Midwest and drop me off on their way to Maryland, when they went on their annual church retreat.

My best times were those summer weeks spent in Washington, D.C. with my favorite aunt. Never married, Delilah McCabe had traveled all over the world and lived for adventure and fun. We explored Mount Vernon, Capitol Hill, Old Town. Every night we ate out in restaurants or bought sandwiches or pizza pies so we didn't have to clean up. Too hot to wash dishes, she would say. She didn't care if I stayed up watching TV and eating ice cream all night, or if I slept until noon. I never had to polish furniture or run the vacuum because she had a maid to do that stuff. A maid!

Best of all for a kid, the ghost lived there.

From the beginning, I'd sensed an otherworldly presence in the apartment. Never anything frightening, but more like someone was guiding me or trying to tell me something. Not exactly the type to dabble in the black arts, Aunt Dee didn't want to talk about it. But she encouraged me to wander the building and ask the neighbors as many questions as I wanted. And I'd heard plenty of rumors from people who worked in the building.

"But that would depend on the ghost," said Jynx. "With this lady last night, you're right. She absolutely does not want these troublemakers in her home, and it's killing her resale."

As Jynx said these words, a lightning-quick current zapped through me—I don't know how else to describe it.

I'm inside that haunted house. In the kitchen, over by the walk-in pantry. A small door opens in the wall, behind shelves. A narrow space. . .

I looked down and it went away.

"But I think Maggie's right about the Blonde in Black. She does lend a certain cachet to the San Leandro. People believe what they want to believe, you know? And they want to keep the Blonde in Black thing going. Like Mag says, it's good for business."

"I heard they had to seal off the roof to keep people away," Stella said. "And that she wanders around on the top floor, looking all romantic and impossibly beautiful."

"What floor is your apartment on?" Nate turned to me. Before I could answer, Mickey squeaked, "OMIGOD! You're on the top floor, aren't you. Oh you are, you are!"

"So what?" I said, my comeback phrase when I don't know what else to say.

"Have you tried to contact her?" Nate asked me.

"I don't exactly have her phone number." Laughter.

"There's a reason why she's still hanging around there, you know. Something's not finished."

"Yeah, like every project I'm working on right now." I

stood to go back to my job as a freelance illustrator. "I gotta get back to work. Thanks for scaring the crap out of me, you guys. Kiss-kiss, everyone."

My first awareness of this gift, or this curse, of what I called my "secret sight" occurred around 1963 when Aunt Delilah had discovered a hidden room behind her huge walk-in closet and decided to convert it into a darkroom. In there, I'd found a page from a yellowed newspaper, folded and tucked into an opening in the wall.

"Look, Aunt Dee." Carefully unfolding it, we saw that it was the Bronx Bee, dated October 12, 1927. The front page had a story about a very wealthy forty-six-year-old man named John "Jack" Stoner who'd been found dead in his apartment. His body had been there for at least a week. Nobody in the building knew him. According to his landlord, Stoner's wife had died and he had moved into the building with his young daughter the year before. There were no surviving relatives, and no mention of what happened to his daughter or his vast fortune.

An inset showed an earlier family portrait; the caption read, "Mr. and Mrs. John Stoner and their daughter, Suzette, c. 1922." The young girl perched on the arm of a velvet-covered chair, leaning slightly toward her mother. Dignified as a banker, ramrod straight, Stoner's black eyes drilled holes into the camera. The way his hand rested possessively on the girl's shoulder, almost forcing her down, made me feel uneasy. Although pretty, the girl's face seemed sad to me.

"Do you know who they are?" I asked my aunt.

"No clue."

"Can I keep it?" I asked.

"Sure."

At that moment, I sort of went numb.

She's in here crying, sick with worry and fright. She knows he's planning something horrible, and she doesn't know how to stop him.

"Maggie?" My aunt had looked concerned, but I hadn't explained. There was no way I could.

During the years since that first episode, there had been several moments where I could see something, almost as a screen unfolds, but I could never will it to happen, or get involved, or do anything other than watch. I still had that newspaper article, tucked in a box in my dresser.

The morning after the coffeehouse episode with Jynx, I walked the fifth floor hallways, looking up until my neck grew stiff. In a deserted back stairwell, I saw a ladder attached to the side of the wall, leading up to nothing.

Probably shouldn't do this, I thought for a second, as I scaled the ladder and climbed toward the ceiling.

I never would have seen the lines in the ceiling if I hadn't been near the top of that ladder. Even though it had been painted over, there was the barest outline of a rectangle. I traced around it with my finger, felt where the nail heads had been covered with paint.

Rushing back to my apartment, I grabbed a flashlight and my tool box. Back in the stairwell, I climbed up again and began to trace around the lines with a putty knife. It took a few minutes to figure out where the nails had been pounded in. I began to dig them out with a hammer, loosening the paint around the sides of the trapdoor.

Yanking hard, I tried to open the trapdoor, but it wouldn't give. I poked around the edges with needle-nose pliers, then pulled until something gave. With a poof of dust, the door creaked open. Paint flakes scattered as I stuck my head up into a large room, which looked like an attic.

Glad I remembered to bring a flashlight. The room was mostly empty, a few boxes piled along the sides. Creeping across the floor, I saw a ray of light along the far wall. As I got closer, I realized that it was a door. It must lead to the roof, I thought, but how to get it open? Just for kicks, I tried the knob. It turned, and the door opened into blinding sunshine.

Like Cary Grant in *To Catch A Thief*, I stepped out and crouched low on the sloping, red-tiled roof. The infamous tower was directly in front of me.

Ignoring the "NO ENTRY" sign, I climbed a flight of worn stone steps up through the tower and came up into an open-air cupola, surrounded by arches. Far below, the Potomac sparkled in the brilliant sunlight, as tiny, gleaming jets approached National Airport, following the winding path of the river. To the right I could see the familiar spires of Georgetown University. Breathtaking.

A short, crumbling wall defined the edges of the cupola. While holding onto the side of an archway, I looked down at the steep, rocky hillside, covered with trees dressed in their winter blacks. Beyond were the rooftops and chimneys of historic Georgetown homes.

Thrilled in a terrified way, standing on top of the world as the wind whipped around the walls, I wondered what chain of events could have brought that desperate young woman to the edge of her life. I pictured her up here—zap!

I see her, standing in the archway, crying. Silently, he comes up from the steps behind her. A man with murder written all over his cruel, handsome face. If only I could warn her! But my mouth won't open and I can't speak or move.

Shaken, I backed up and sat down. After a few minutes, I stood and worked my way back toward my apartment.

Verna, the resident manager, was yapping on the phone. The royal guardswoman. She did a wonderful job, keeping the corridors of the San Leandro safe from all kinds of stupid, annoying people.

Enormous, immovable, and implacable, Verna had been right beside Aunt Delilah's bedside through the last days of her life, taking her hot soup and pots of Earl Gray tea, making her as comfortable as possible, reading to her, playing cards when Aunt Dee felt strong enough.

Seeing me, Verna smiled as she hung up. "Hey, darlin', what's hap'nin'?"

"Hi, Verna. Just a question. Who's the best person to talk to about history of the San Leandro?"

"Used to be Mr. McKittrick, but he's got the Big A and he don't remember nothin'. His daughter moved in to take care of him. He don't even know where he's at most of the time."

"Oh, poor man." And his poor daughter, I thought. "Anybody else who might know?"

"There was one lady who lived here forever, until they moved her over to Fordham."

I recognized the name as an assisted-living facility on Dent Place. "What's her name?"

"Mrs. Clinton, sumpin' like that. She's batty, too." With her right index finger, Verna drew circles beside her temple. "I want somebody to just shoot me when I get to be that old."

"Thanks, Verna."

Like a dinner guest who thoroughly enjoyed the evening, autumn lingered late in D.C. Leaves of gold and red carpeted the streets and sidewalks, and sunlight warmed the air. Beautiful afternoon for a walk to the Georgetown public library, where light poured in through story-high windows. People sat reading at wooden tables, and others were nestled cozily in window seats. No crazy people ranting on about the state of the world today.

The Peabody Room held an excellent collection of historical Georgetown books and papers, where I discovered that the San Leandro had been converted from a private residence to a hotel around 1902, then divided into luxury apartments in 1928–29. If Nick and Nora Charles had landed in D.C. instead of San Francisco, they would have lived in a fabulous flat in the San Leandro. In the early 1970s, new owners remodeled the entire complex.

I asked the librarian if there were any books or magazines about ghosts in Georgetown. Looking over her glasses at me, she pointed to a solid wall of oak bookcases with glass doors, each case packed with books.

"Which one has the ghost stuff?"

"They all do."

Nearly every place in Georgetown claimed to be haunted, especially the Old Stone House on M Street, verified by ghost experts as having at least seven spirits in residence. After wondering about the qualifications required for being a ghost expert, I searched for more than an hour and finally hit the jackpot. A local magazine from 1946 had a full-page photo of the San Leandro showing the tower and the craggy hillside below. The headline read: "San Leandro Residents Shocked at Tragic Death of Young Bride."

On the next page were wedding photos of a gorgeous young woman with cascading blonde hair, dressed in a street-length suit and black and white spectator pumps, standing next to her dark-haired, dashing groom. Nearby stood another strikingly beautiful young woman. The caption read: "Amelia Beatrice Clifton married Louis Sanford of California. Suzette Clifton, the bride's mother (at left), gave the wedding."

Whoa. That young thing is the mother? She looked a lot more like a sister. Must have been a child bride.

After the honeymoon, the newlyweds moved in with Amelia's mother, who had an apartment in the San Leandro. Within six months, 19-year old Amelia killed herself. Official cause of death: suicide.

During the condo conversion of 1970–71, people began to report sightings of the Blonde in Black. Construction had been delayed after tools were found in different places, supplies disappeared, and doors and windows were found standing open after having been locked the night before. Dozens of laborers claimed to have seen an apparition in black wandering through the hallways up on the top floor, and they refused to go there to work.

I copied the magazine article and raced back home.

Old homes in Georgetown held onto secrets. Even though the outside structures might have been totally remodeled, the heart of the home was still a mystery. I remembered the kitchen that had flashed in my brain the other night, when I'd been looking at Jynx.

Early the next morning, I called her. "Listen, don't ask me any questions, but you know your author's house with the poltergeists?"

"Yeah?" she said.

"Well, is it possible that her son's behind everything?"

"Maggie, I swear he's doing it all, and his little friend is in on it with him. But I don't know how to prove it. I've looked for secret rooms, hidden staircases, all that jazz. Can't find anything."

"Listen, is there a walk-in pantry in the kitchen?"

Pause. "Yes. How did you know that?"

"Look behind the pantry shelves. I think there's a dumb-waiter in the wall there."

A dumbwaiter was like a tiny elevator, a movable box in the wall with shelves for carrying food and dishes between floors. Just big enough for a kid.

I heard her take in a sharp breath. "I never thought of that. You want to explain how you did?"

"I'm not sure I can right now, Jynx."

"We'll have to talk sometime, girlfriend. But first, thank you so much. I'll go back there today."

Later that morning, I walked over to Dent Place and found the Fordham. An old mansion that had been beautifully restored, it had a ramp for wheelchair access, smooth wooden floors underneath the carpets, wide hallways and large elevators. The grounds were immaculately tended, with late fall flowers still in bloom. After walking down a long, narrow entrance hall and turning left, I found a reception desk tucked into an alcove.

"Hi, I'm Maggie McCabe. Does a Mrs. Clinton live here?" I asked a young woman with big, pouffy hair.

"No, there's no one here by that name," she said. Something about her smelled like a vanilla candle.

"Are you sure? I heard from a very reliable source that she lived here. She moved over from the San Leandro, that big place up on the hill," I said, pointing back as though that would clarify everything. "Could you just check with someone?"

"Oh, wait a sec. You mean Mrs. Clifton?"

"The name clicked and pieces went together. Yeah, that's it." Suzette Clifton, mother of the Blonde in Black, lived right here. Excited now, I felt the hair stand up on my arms. "Can I see her?"

"Well, actually, she died," said Ms. Pouffy Hair, cracking her chewing gum.

"Oh, no! When?"

"Just a day or so ago, actually." Gum snapped.

Another woman had come up behind the desk. Elegantly dressed in a gray tweed suit, her silver hair cut short and blunt, she spoke softly but firmly. "Brittney, would you please go check on the set-up for our ten o'clock? Thank you."

Brittney left. Turning to me, the older woman smiled and extended her hand. "I'm Evangeline Morris, director of Fordham. Can I help you?"

"I hope so. I just heard—"

"Yes, I'm so sorry you had to hear that way. Were you related to Mrs. Clifton?" Evangeline Morris's eyes looked kind.

"No, I didn't know her. But I wanted to meet her."

"Oh, I see. Well, she was one of our most beloved residents. She'll certainly be missed around here."

"How did she die?"

"I'm sorry, I can't divulge that information to anyone except the family."

"Are her things still in her room? Or has everything been taken away?"

"It's been thoroughly cleaned." She glanced at her watch.

"Could I just peek in?" I pleaded. "Look, I live in the San Leandro, in the apartment where she used to live. I'm just trying to figure out an old mystery involving the Blonde in Black. I'm not sure what I'm even looking for, but I think she would've helped me."

"Yes, I'm sure she would have, but I can't make an exception. Rules, you know. Sorry. Good day." Those lovely eyes had changed to cold gunmetal gray.

I walked outside, feeling sad and yet strangely relieved. Was it a coincidence that the mother of the Blonde in Black had died right when all these visions were coming to me? Or could it be possible that she felt able to let go, now that I accepted, if not quite understood, my gift of secret sight?

Events of the past few days had given me hope that I would finally be able to understand why I heard and saw things that no one else did. But with the only person who knew the truth about the Blonde in Black now gone, would I ever know the rest of the story?

Turning to the left, I headed toward Thirtieth Street and the climb back up the hill. On Thirtieth, I saw a red GTI, following me slowly.

I panicked and picked up my speed. The car moved a bit faster. What's going on here?

"Miss McCabe!" I heard a voice calling out. I turned and looked. Brittney sat in her car, motioning for me to get in. I did and we drove up to R Street, where she parked and turned off the engine.

"I could actually lose my job over this," Brittney said, cracking her gum.

"What do you mean?"

"By telling you the truth about sweet old Mrs. Clifton. We're not supposed to talk about our residents, but she's gone now, and somebody's gotta know the real deal."

"Good move, Brittney," I said.

"Everybody thought she was crazy, but she wasn't, believe me. Nobody ever listened to her, besides me, that is. We got really close after my grandmother died. She always said that if anyone ever asked about the Blonde in Black, I should tell them about the murders."

"What are you talking about?"

"You know, she was so sweet, it's hard to believe she could've killed anyone. Not that she was sorry about it, because they both totally deserved it, but a long time ago she killed two men," Brittney said. "I didn't believe her at first, but after she told me why she had to do them, well, I would've done it, too."

"Who were they?"

"She killed Louis, her son-in-law, because he murdered her daughter, Amelia. She got, like, a million dollars from her father's estate on her wedding day, and Louis wanted it all. Pushed her over the edge of that tower up there, made it look like suicide. But Mrs. Clifton killed him that same night. Whacked him with a poker and dragged his body down to the furnace. They never found a trace of him."

The face I'd seen, high atop the San Leandro tower yesterday, belonged to Louis Sanford. He'd climbed up to that roof sixty years ago to murder his young bride.

"And the other man?" I asked, but I already knew.

"Well, it was her father. Like, even before her mother died, her father actually, you know, raped her. Not just once, but a lot of times. She couldn't tell anybody, and he wouldn't stop, so she had to kill him."

"It was different for kids then," I said. "No help networks like we have today. What an amazing woman she must have been." Suzette Clifton had managed to give me the final piece of the puzzle by sharing it with Brittney. Now that I knew the truth, and it would not die with Suzette.

However she'd managed to get away with his murder, it was pretty smart for a young girl of seventeen or eighteen. She must have been desperate when she found out she was pregnant, knew that he would never let her go as long as he was alive, realized she had to get rid of him forever.

John "Jack" Stoner, whose photo I'd seen in the old newspaper in my aunt's apartment years ago, wasn't just Suzette's father—he'd also fathered her daughter, the Blonde in Black.

Sandi Wilson is the author of Be the Boss: Start and Run Your Own Service Business *(Avon, 1985), and* Be the Boss II: Running A Successful Service Business *(Avon, 1993), and more than fifty freelance articles. Her books have sold more than 100,000 copies. She and her partner have owned a D.C.-based electronic design studio for twenty-five years. Wilson is working*

Sandi Wilson

on a mystery series featuring the Blonde in Black. She loves dancing and yoga, is terrible at tennis, and fairly famous for her double chocolate chip cookies.